Burnell Pannill

LIKE BIRDS, LIKE FISHES
and Other Stories

LIKE BIRDS, LIKE FISHES
and Other Stories

R. PRAWER JHABVALA

W · W · NORTON & COMPANY · INC ·
NEW YORK

FOR
JIM AND ISMAIL

THE FOLLOWING stories appeared originally in *The New Yorker:* THE OLD LADY, THE WIDOW, THE INTERVIEW, A BIRTHDAY IN LONDON, LEKHA, and SIXTH CHILD. MY FIRST MARRIAGE first appeared in *Encounter,* and is reprinted with their permission. Acknowledgments are due also to *Yale Review,* who published A LOSS OF FAITH and THE ALIENS, and to *Kenyon Review,* who published THE AWARD.

CONTENTS

THE OLD LADY 9

A LOSS OF FAITH 23

THE AWARD 45

THE WIDOW 60

THE ALIENS 84

THE INTERVIEW 107

A BIRTHDAY IN LONDON 123

LIKE BIRDS, LIKE FISHES 140

LEKHA 166

SIXTH CHILD 189

MY FIRST MARRIAGE 203

THE OLD LADY

SHE woke up, as she did every morning, very early and very happy. The sky was still grey, and only here and there a bird stirred in a tree and gave its first, fresh twitter. She stood on her veranda and looked out at this quiet dawn and smiled with happiness. She was strong and calm and at peace. Still smiling, she turned back into her bedroom and sat on the floor before the little table on which stood the small brass image of Vishnu and an incense holder and a framed photograph of her guru. She sat there with her legs crossed under her and her hands laid palm upwards on her knees. She sat like that for quite a long time, though she did not know for how long, because she was too happy to be aware of any time.

Then the bearer came in with her morning tea, set out on her silver tray, and she smiled and was happy at that too, because she always enjoyed her morning tea. Munni, her grand-daughter, came with her tumbler of milk, and they sat drinking together. Munni told her dream – she had a dream every night – this time about how a big white horse had come for her and carried her off to a blue cloud. 'How beautiful,' said her grandmother admiringly, and Munni said in a complacently off-hand way that yes, it was. Sometimes Munni's dreams were beautiful and fantastic, and sometimes they were very stern and tragic, as when she dreamed that both her parents had been condemned to be hanged and she had watched the execution. Her grand-mother was always the first person to be informed of these

dreams, and afterwards they sat and discussed them together. Nobody else in the house would listen to Munni's
dreams, but her grandmother told her they were serious and
important.

Leila and Bobo always liked to sleep a long time, so the
old lady had time to go round and see that everything was
being properly cleaned and dusted. The whole house was
alive with cleaning: marble floors were washed, brass ornaments rubbed, rugs beaten, cushions shaken, door handles
polished, fresh flowers put in vases. The old lady walked
around sprinkling rosewater out of a long-handled silver
sprinkler; she sang as she did so, she was feeling so happy
and lighthearted – like a bird, she thought, she felt just like
a bird singing from green trees and lawns on a dewy
morning.

But her daughter Leila was feeling cross. She suffered
from some stomach trouble, and that always made her
irritable in the mornings. She had consulted many doctors,
but they all said that there was nothing wrong. 'It is nerves,'
they told her. So now Leila often referred to her nerves.

'I can't bear it,' was the first thing she said, and her
mother asked: 'What, daughter?' full of sympathy. Leila's
face was an unhealthy colour and it was screwed up with
irritation and her breath did not smell very nice. Looking
at her, the old lady was a little ashamed that she herself
was feeling so fresh and gay.

'Not today,' said Leila, shutting her eyes. 'I can't bear it
today. He will talk, and we will all talk, and what will be
the good of it?'

'Krishna?' said her mother. Leila nodded, her eyes still
painfully shut. Her mother clicked her tongue in sympathy
but nevertheless offered, 'It will be nice to see him.' Leila
laughed hollowly.

Munni asked, 'Daddy is coming today?'

'Go away and play,' Leila told her; Munni saw that her mother was in her morning mood, so she went without comment.

'And it will be nice to see him eat,' the old lady said, a trifle sadly. She never could help feeling sorry for her son-in-law. 'I don't know *what* they give him in that hotel.' She added, 'Poor boy,' and could not suppress a very gentle sigh.

'Oh, Mother,' said Leila in exasperation.

'I know, I know,' said the old lady. 'It is not your fault.' Now she felt sorry for both of them, for Krishna and for Leila. How sad it was for people to be unhappy in their marriage. She sighed, and picked up a plate of biscuits. She took the plate into the drawing-room and put it on a table beside her son Bobo, who lay stretched out on the sofa, reading an art magazine. She enjoyed feeding biscuits to Bobo – she had baked them herself, with such love – but she wished he were not getting so fat. His stomach bulged through his silk shirt, his cheeks were round and puffed. It was not a healthy fatness, and one could see that he often had pimples and boils.

The old lady hurried out into the garden. She had to hurry because she felt waves of happiness passing over her: not really happiness, but that was what she called it to herself, because she knew no other word for it. She stood in the garden, sheltered from the morning sun by the tall old trees, and the birds' twittering trickled like water, and the gardener's hose gurgled softly in the grass, and she could hear the gardener snipping with his shears. She stood there with her eyes shut, seeing nothing, yet feeling everything, while ecstasy held her and carried her. She did not mind the gardener seeing her like this – though she did mind her children seeing. That was why she always hurried away from them when she felt her happiness coming over her. She did not want them to know about it. Perhaps because she felt guilty for having something so precious and not being able to share it with them.

Munni came running across the lawn, with her doll pushed carelessly under her arm; one finger was stuck in her mouth and she was warbling a war song. She ran straight into her grandmother and, clasping her arms round the old lady's legs, buried her face in the sari, which smelled of jasmine scent and camphor. The old lady laughed happily. Once the transition from her states of ecstasy had been very difficult for her, but now it was easy and effortless. Everything now was easy and effortless. Gay as a young girl, she went back to the house and into the kitchen, where the cook sat squatting on the floor and vigorously ground spices on a stone. 'Quickly now!' the old lady cried in her bright voice. 'Cut up the onions!' and she began to melt fat in a pan, deftly shaking it round with sharp little jerks. She had always loved cooking.

The cook let his knife slice through an onion with precision, his head laid critically to one side. 'Have you heard?' he said. 'Yesterday they killed a snake outside Mathur Sahib's bungalow.'

'A snake!' she cried.

'A cobra,' he said with relish, handing her the onions which she slid into the fat while clicking her tongue over the cobra. 'It was so long,' he told her, showing her with his hands; he pursed his mouth and said in a judicious voice, 'It must have been some evil spirit.'

'Yes,' she said, 'it is difficult to know in what shape an evil spirit may not come to visit us. Are the spices ready?'

·   ·   ·   ·   ·

'Mother!' Leila called from the drawing-room and was annoyed when her mother failed to hear her. 'She must be gossiping with the servants again,' she told Bobo who smiled indulgently and said, 'Why not, if it makes her happy?'

'I know,' said Leila, 'but it is hardly dignified.'

Bobo was looking at some Rajput miniatures. 'Lovely,' he murmured with sensuousness, trying to enjoy them like a taste.

'Mother is often not dignified,' Leila said. 'For instance, with Krishna. It is very awkward for me when she is so soft with Krishna.'

'Lovely,' said Bobo, 'but probably fake.' He looked up to ask : 'Why awkward?'

'It might make Krishna think – you see,' she said with emphasis, 'I want it to be *quite* clear that everything is finished and there can be no reconciliation.'

'But isn't that obvious? When you and Munni are living here —'

'But Mother keeps calling him!' Leila cried in exasperation. 'When none of us is at home, she goes quietly to the telephone and says Krishna, come and eat a meal with us.'

'Poor fellow,' murmured Bobo, who had inherited some part of his mother's sympathy.

'Yes, but what about me!' Leila demanded. 'Because you and Mother feel sorry for him, you want me always to be tied to an incompatible husband?'

Bobo yawned (how he hated argument! and his sister was very argumentative) but politely tried to cover it up.

'It is very difficult for me,' sighed Leila, and then she said, 'I am going to telephone.'

Her mother, emerging from the kitchen, was glad to see her telephoning. She knew that Leila's mood always improved at the telephone. Already her voice was quite cheerful: 'We shall just have to call an Extraordinary Meeting, that's all,' she was saying. Her telephone conversations were full of references to meetings, sub-committees, resolutions, agendas. She was an enthusiastic committee woman and had many committee friends, to whom she telephoned and with whom she exchanged, several times a day, important notes and papers, which were carried to and fro by a scared young clerk specially hired for the purpose.

'Leila was complaining that you gossip too much with the servants,' Bobo told the old lady. He said it with good humour, but nevertheless in that patronizing tone which all her children used towards her. The old lady did not mind. On the contrary, she rather liked being patronized by her children. They were so much cleverer than she had ever been.

'Yes,' she said, smiling radiantly, 'I talk too much. Shall I bring your milk?' And then she said, 'Oh son, why won't you get married?' She did so want him to. But Bobo only smiled, showing his pointed wide-spaced little teeth and his gums. She sat down and said dreamily, 'I wish one of you two boys would get married. I could arrange so nicely for you.' She could talk like this to Bobo, though not to her other son. If she diffidently mentioned marriage to Satish, he only clicked his tongue and made a movement of irritation.

'And you would be happy,' she told Bobo, looking at him with appealing eyes. 'With a wife and children you would be so happy.' And maybe with a wife and children he would become more active and would no longer lie all day on a sofa, reading and looking at *objets d'art*. Of course, she realized that was his work, and she was always proud when an article of his appeared in one of the art magazines or in the Sunday edition of the *Statesman*. But still, she did wish he would *move* a little more; if only to stop him from getting too fat.

'Why not talk to Satish?' Bobo teased her.

She shrugged. 'He is so busy, poor boy,' she murmured.

'So busy making money and a name,' Bobo said, a trifle acidly. The two brothers did not get on well together. Satish had taken very much after his father; like his father, he had gone in for law and had already established a very remunerative practice for himself. He was hardworking and ambitious, which Bobo decidedly was not.

Krishna turned up punctually at lunchtime. He was nervous, and so was giggling in that rather silly way he had. The old lady glanced apprehensively at Leila and saw, as she had feared and expected, that Leila was already looking irritated. Krishna must also have noticed, for he giggled more; and then, feeling obliged to make some remark, made this: 'Hot again today, no?'

'Yes!' cried the old lady, so eager that her voice trembled. 'Yes, hot!' Now Leila was frowning at her mother too. Bobo, still lying on the sofa with a big, glossy art magazine, said, 'Are we going to discuss the weather?' Krishna laughed out loud. Munni came in and said, 'Oh look, Daddy has come.' Her grandmother would have liked to see her greet him more warmly, but Munni made no further move towards him. Krishna looked over his daughter's head, pretending in his shyness not to see her.

They were already seated round the huge, heavy-legged dining-table when Satish came in, saying briskly 'Sorry I'm late.' This briskness and his hasty entrance, combined with a frowning air of preoccupation, were enough to make them all feel ashamed of their idleness, which had allowed them to sit down, spaciously and in good time, for their lunch. The old lady got up, flustered and hurried; she seized the tray from the bearer who was serving them and began herself to fill her son's plate. Satish let her serve him but said, 'Why do you fuss so, Mother?' in a calm, patronizing voice.

'Allow me, son,' she said, her hands shaking a little as she piled food on to his plate, 'it is my pleasure.' Satish was so much like his father that she even felt towards him as she used to feel towards her husband: inadequate, that is, and as if she had neglected some part of her duty. Only then, in her youth and middle age, this feeling had penetrated her completely, so that she had felt dissatisfied and unhappy, whereas now it was only a kind of surface disturbance, which left her great depths of calm unrippled. Perhaps she was even glad of this disturbance, and tended slightly to exaggerate it; because it made her feel that she was still sufficiently in touch with her children and had not yet given herself over to her own happiness alone.

After a while Satish said, 'Well, if you want to file your divorce papers, you had better make up your minds.'

Leila said at once, 'How long have I been telling you that my mind *is* made up.' So then they all looked at Krishna, who became so confused that he giggled, and that confused him further, so that with flushed face he bent close over his plate and ate. The old lady called quite sharply to the bearer, 'Give Krishna Sahib water! Don't you see his glass is empty?'

'It is better to get these things over and done with,' said Satish in his brisk, busy voice.

Bobo drawled in deliberate contrast: 'Don't hurry them into something they might not wish to do.'

'There is no question,' said Leila, 'of *not* wishing.'

Bobo shrugged and waved his hand to the bearer to bring the rice round again.

'What are divorce papers?' Munni whispered to her grandmother.

Leila said in a loud voice, 'Mother, please don't encourage Munni to speak before everything on her plate is finished.'

'Eat, child, eat,' the old lady obediently murmured. She remembered so many meals in this room round this table: her husband stern and domineering like Satish, her children tense with conflict. And she herself full of unhappiness, because she did not know what to do or what to say. She still did not know what to do or what to say; but now she was only gently sad because she could not show her children the way to her own peace.

'Anywhere else,' said Leila fiercely, 'everything would have been settled and finished long ago.'

'Now we shall hear about poor oppressed Indian womanhood,' Bobo said with a smile.

'For you everything is a joke,' Leila accused him. 'But it is true. In Europe and America —'

'Why don't we remain to the point?' said Satish shortly.

'It *is* the point!' Leila said. 'Our attitude of mind is wrong. We don't understand that divorce is a natural thing in any enlightened society.'

And Krishna was as shy and embarrassed as a young girl, picking at his food with the point of his fork, his eyes lowered.

'Yes, yes,' said Satish, 'but what is it you want to *do*?'

Munni looked up from her plate. She was a little afraid of her uncle Satish, but she found him interesting. For instance, she found it interesting that he should suggest doing something; she liked to hear such talk, it offered possibilities. Nothing of what the others talked ever offered possibilities – that was why she usually did not bother to listen to them.

'But I have told you,' Leila said.

'Oh no, not again,' said Bobo, peering into the bowl of dessert the bearer was offering to him, and then casting an accusing look at his mother.

'Tomorrow I will make carrot halwa,' she promised him.

'And you, Krishna?' Satish said, now looking directly at his brother-in-law who, thus forced to commit himself, glanced first helplessly round the table. His mother-in-law smiled at him encouragingly, but he was too nervous to smile back.

'Yes,' he said at last. 'Of course.'

There was a silence. The old lady tried hard to think of something suitable to interpose, but it was Leila who spoke first. 'Really!' she said in an exasperation which was however half triumphant, for after all her point was being proved.

'Of course,' said Krishna with a heroic effort, 'if Leila wants . . .' He looked distressed. 'Of course,' he said again, 'if she wants,' and then he giggled and quickly continued to eat. The old lady felt that she loved him terribly. Leila put both her hands to her forehead and said, 'This is frightful for my nerves.'

Afterwards Satish paced up and down the drawing-room, looking at his watch and saying, 'I have just half an hour.' Bobo, replete and drowsy with food, was again lying on the sofa and leafing through a magazine with a dreamy smile on his lips. A note had just come for Leila and she sat on the edge of a chair and opened it; she frowned and pursed her lips and looked busy, while the young clerk who had brought it stood in front of her with his head bent. Everybody seemed to be waiting for something.

The old lady got up and hurried to her room. Only for one minute, she promised herself. She sat in front of the little table with the image of Vishnu and the photograph of her guru, and – God forgive her – at once forgot all about her children sitting puzzled in the drawing-room. Everything now was clear and serene. Her guru looked at her out of his silver frame: he had large burning eyes and an ugly mouth with thick unshaped lips. The very first time she had seen him, she had known that he was the man who would guide her. Not much had been said. She had gone to see him with a friend. He sat in a little room over a sweetmeat shop. There were several other people in the room, sitting around, not doing anything much. Out on the veranda, which overlooked the street, a woman sat cooking and a fat naked little boy sat beside her and watched. Her friend had asked the guru several questions, but he had only smiled instead of replying. Then suddenly he had turned, not to her friend but to her, and his eyes burned as he looked at her and he said, 'If you look for it, peace is not hard to find.' So now she sat crosslegged before her little table, surrounded by vast fields of peace in which her spirit frisked like a lamb. While downstairs in the drawing-room Bobo yawned and said, 'Where is Mother?' hard put to it to suppress a burp.

'Why does she always disappear like that?' Leila said. She licked the flap of an envelope in an efficient way and handed it to the clerk, who still stood humbly before her; she said, 'Now see that you deliver this at once, but at *once*,' sharply.

'Perhaps she is resting?' Krishna diffidently suggested.

'Poor Mother,' Bobo said. They often said 'poor Mother', for they felt she ought to be in need of pity. Their father had always been the strong force in the family, and it was only to be expected that after his death she should be lost and broken. That was why they said 'poor Mother' and, when they remembered, were kind and considerate to her.

'Yes, but since we are here to *discuss*,' Leila said, and Krishna again looked embarrassed. Satish flicked out his wrist to look at his watch; he frowned, and managed to look pressed for time. Bobo, observing him, put on a deliberate gentleman-of-leisure act, crossing his plump legs one over the other as he lay on the sofa.

Munni quietly crept up the stairs and into her grandmother's room. She came up behind the old lady and put her arms round her neck and whispered into her ear, 'They are all waiting for you.' But Grandmother did not move. Maybe she was dead. Munni peered round into her face. Grandmother's eyes were wide open, and her mouth too was slightly open, with the tip of the tongue showing. She looked very strange. What if she really was dead? They would put a red cloth over her and carry her on a board down to the Jumna and there they would burn her till there was nothing left of her but ashes. 'Grandmother!' Munni suddenly cried. The old lady said, 'Yes, Munni' in a quiet voice.

After a while Munni said, 'When people get very, very, *very* old, do they die?'

'Yes,' said the old lady cheerfully, 'they die.'

There was another pause, and then Munni asked: 'Grandmother, are you very, very, *very* old?'

'Oh yes,' said the old lady, even more cheerfully.

'No!' Munni cried angrily. 'The cook's mother is much older than you are! I know!'

The old lady smiled and began to stroke Munni's hair. They sat like that together, and the guru looked at them from out of the photograph.

'When people die,' the old lady said, 'they become happy.'

'But they are burnt, how can they be happy?'

'Their spirit is happy,' the old lady explained; and she smiled, her eyes looking far into the distance as if she saw there vast flowering plains for spirits to be happy in.

When they got downstairs, Satish said with an air of finality, 'Well, I have to be going,' and slapped his pocket to see if his car key was in it.

'Already?' said the old lady in a somewhat dazed manner. She was blinking her eyes as if she had just woken up, which made Leila say, 'Really, Mother, you could have postponed your nap for *one* afternoon.' Her mother at once looked contrite and blamed herself for selfishness.

'Nothing settled, as usual,' Satish said. 'If only you people would let me know what you want.'

'But I have told you!' Leila cried. Krishna bent his head and pretended to be engrossed in the back page of a folded newspaper.

The old lady ventured to say, 'Perhaps it would be better to wait.' Her voice was cracked and nervous, and after she had spoken there was a silence, so that she wished she had not spoken.

'Mother doesn't understand,' Leila at last said. 'She still thinks the marriage bond is sacred'; and she made a school-girl face of distaste to show how completely she dissociated herself from such an attitude.

Bobo said, 'You can't expect Mother to give up the ideas of her generation so easily.'

'No,' said Leila, 'but that is no reason why she should criticize *our* ideas.'

The old lady sat humbly with her hands folded in her lap and listened to them talking about her. She thought they were right and that she was old-fashioned, with no conception of the modern ideas and principles which guided their lives. She admired her children for being so much more advanced and intelligent than she was; but that did not prevent her from feeling sorry for them. If only she could have shown them – opened the way for them as it had been opened for herself that day in the shabby little room where people sat around casually and the smell of cooking came from the veranda.

'You can give me a lift in your car,' Leila told Satish. 'I have a meeting.'

Krishna got up at once and said, 'Let me.' His eyes and voice begged quite without shame. But Leila turned away from him and followed Satish. Krishna sat down again, looking unhappy.

Perhaps she could show Krishna. She looked at him tenderly and thought that perhaps she loved him best of all. Bobo had gone to sleep on the sofa. His heavy head had dropped sideways and his mouth was slightly open to allow big regular breaths to escape. The old lady put out one finger and laid it on Krishna's wrist. What she had to communicate could not be said in words. But she felt him to be ready for it: he was unhappy and tender and lost. She could feel him seeking for something, straining for something, without himself knowing it. She wanted to pray to be able to help him. Slowly she stroked his wrist with her finger. Come with me, she wanted to say.

'Grandmother,' Munni said sternly, watching the old lady stroke Krishna's wrist, 'you know very well Mummy says we mustn't be too kind to Daddy.'

A LOSS OF FAITH

RAM KUMAR could not remember his father who had been a printer and had died of a sudden fever, leaving his wife and five small children to be supported by his brother, a postal inspector. The impression that Ram Kumar's mother gave of her husband was, on the one hand, that of a man all tenderness and generosity and, on the other, of one very much like his brother the postal inspector – that is to say, a man who was often drunk on raw liquor, was careless of his family and beat his wife. In her moments of depression – which were frequent, for her life among her sisters-in-law and mother-in-law was not easy – she favoured the first impression: 'Ah,' she would say, 'if my children's father were still alive, it would be different for me'; and then she would suggest how her husband in his lifetime had cared for her, brought special foods for her when she was pregnant, given her and the children warm things to wear in the winter, and on festival days had taken them to see fairs and processions. But when things were not going too badly for her, she gave a different picture. Then she spoke with a kind of bitter satisfaction of the way all men were the same, all given to drink, selfishness and wife-beating; and she compressed her lips and nodded her head up and down, suggesting that, if called upon, she could tell many a tale from her own experience of married life to illustrate this truth.

Her eldest child – not Ram Kumar, who was the third – was fortunately a boy, and all her hope was in him. Vijay was a strong, healthy, daring boy, and she could hardly wait for him to grow up and earn money and take her and her other children away to live with him. But when he finally did grow up, he turned out to be too fond of strolling through the bazaars, going to the cinema and having fun with his friends to give much of his attention to the jobs that were found for him; so that within two years he had run through fourteen such jobs – all of the nature of office messenger or contractor's errand boy – and it became clear even to his mother that he would not hurriedly earn a lot of money. After these two years, he disappeared and was not heard of for another two; at the end of which time he came back and said he had been to Calcutta, where he had earned a lot of money and had been about to send for them when a thief had come in the night and stolen it all from under his bed. He was now in no hurry to look for another job, but stayed around in his uncle's home during the day and went out towards evening to enjoy life with his numerous acquaintances.

At first he went out quite often with his uncle and the two came back late in the night, very drunk and very friendly. But the friendship did not last long, and soon the uncle came to be tired of feeding a large, strong, healthy nephew who made no attempts to find another job. Quarrels between them became more and more frequent: watched by women cowering against the wall and clutching their hair, the two of them flung bitter words against one another; until one day the nephew ended another such quarrel by smashing his fist in his uncle's face and, stepping over the prostrate body, disappeared out of the house. When he next reappeared, he was wearing a beautiful suit of smuggled silk and a big ring on his little finger and was working in some rather shady capacity for a big business magnate. But though he now really seemed to be earning a lot of money, he made no attempts to take away his mother and his younger brother and sisters. Nor did he come to see them very often or, when he did, speak much of his affairs; so that it was only by devious routes that they finally discovered him to be spending much of his time and most of his money on a very beautiful young Muslim lady, who employed her abilities at singing and dancing to entertain at certain kinds of parties. His mother took this news as she had taken all her other afflictions: with tears, with resignation, with pleas to God to lighten her lot.

Meanwhile Ram Kumar too was growing up, and his mother tried to turn her hopes to him. But, unlike his brother, he was not very promising. Where Vijay was broad and strong and good-looking, Ram Kumar was small and weak, with a pinched face to go with his pinched body. And he was always afraid. At the little charity school he attended he was afraid both of the master and of the other boys. He worked feverishly so that the master should have nothing with which to reproach him, and he hunched himself up to an even smaller size in the hope that the boys would not notice him. He was so successful that nobody, neither master nor boys, ever did notice him, and he remained unknown, unbefriended and – which was what he had aimed for – unmolested.

At home he tried the same tactics, though less successfully. The whole family lived together in one room and one veranda. There were Ram Kumar, his mother and his two sisters – his elder sister had been married to a policeman in Saharanpur, and Vijay, of course was no longer living with them – the postal inspector uncle with his wife and children, as well as one widowed aunt and a grandmother. Their room was in a row of six quarters built on one side of a courtyard which had on its other side the workshop of a dry-cleaner and the office with cyclostyle of an Urdu weekly of limited circulation. On summer nights all the families slept outside in the courtyard, but summer days were hot and long and the room small, and even Ram Kumar could not always escape notice. He suffered especially from his thin, hard, old grandmother and the widowed aunt, who looked just as old as the grandmother. They were often angry with him and beat him and abused him, while he cowered in a corner and wept into his hands.

There was no one who could protect him against them. His mother could not even put in a good word for him because, if she had done so, they would have begun to beat and abuse her too. As it was, they did this often enough. They pinched her and pulled her hair and poked her with sharp cooking-irons. 'Evil eye,' they called her, 'killer of your husband, bringer of death.' She had to accept everything, for it was true she was a widow and guilty of the sin of outliving her husband. Ram Kumar had to watch the beatings meted out to his mother as she had to watch his; but it did not bring him any closer to her. On the contrary, he even resented her because she was weak and could not protect him. So when she tried to comfort him after his beatings, petting and stroking and whispering to him, he sat there passive and unmoved with his face closed and the tear-marks on his cheeks; and when she whispered into his ear, 'When you are grown-up and are earning a lot of money, you will take me away to live with you,' he did not reply and even tightened his lips, for though he had, in his wilder moments, hopes of going away himself, he never entertained the idea of taking her with him.

He liked to sit on the opposite side of their courtyard, in the poky little office of the old man who wrote, cyclostyled and distributed the Urdu weekly. The old man sat on the floor with a tiny desk in front of him and lingered lovingly with a quill pen over the flowering Urdu script in which he wrote his paper. Ram Kumar was not interested in what he was writing, but he liked the peace and order of the little room – the smell of black ink and the gentle sucking noise the old man made between his teeth as he wrote. Very few visitors ever came to disturb him; but it was through one such visitor, a relative of the old man's, that Ram Kumar got a job. It happened that the relative sat talking to the old man about this and that – a sick sister, a journey to Lucknow – and mentioned in passing that a boy was wanted to help in the shop in which he was employed. The old man jerked his head back to where Ram Kumar sat quietly behind the cyclostyle and said, 'Take him.' Ram Kumar was startled: he was not used to the old man taking any notice of him. But that 'Take him' came at a right time. He had left school, his uncle was trying to find him a job, his grandmother and aunt abused him for being idle. So he went gratefully to the shop.

He loved it from the first. It was a draper and outfitter's shop, but not an ordinary shop, not one of the little booths in the city bazaars which was the only kind of shop he and his like ever visited. This was in the fashionable shopping centre of New Delhi, where the rich went, and it was a big shop with a door to go in by and two glass windows in which were displayed samples of all the beautiful things sold inside. There were two counters inside, and behind the counters stood the assistants, serving the customers. Ram Kumar watched them with eager eyes, he darted forward to be of assistance to them in taking the goods from the shelves, his lips moved with theirs as they offered the customers all there was at their disposal. It did not take him long to know more about stock and prices than any other employee in the shop; for though he was only the general boy, hired to go out on errands, wrap parcels and tidy up counters, he had soon learnt so much that the others began to rely on him, and it was he who was asked, 'Ram Kumar, has the new voile come in yet?' 'Ram Kumar, is there a baby vest, size 2?' 'Ram Kumar, how much for Hind Mill sheets, single-bed size?'

After about a year, they began to allow him to change the goods in the windows. He spent sweet hours displaying newly arrived stock, not with taste but with love; reverently he laid out or hung up materials, blankets, ladies' underwear and children's clothing. Inside the shop, on the edge of one of the counters, stood a pale wax doll, two feet high and rather peeling, with a mouse-tooth smile, one hand with a finger missing outstretched, its feet painted with white socks and black anklestrap shoes. Once a week, Ram Kumar changed its clothes, making it display now a pink satin frock with lace trimmings, now a boy's sailor suit or a hand-embroidered skirt with cap to match. He loved the doll and loved dressing it, but there was no element of play in the way he handled it; this was work for him, something important and deadly earnest.

He did not spend much time at home any more. He left early in the morning, carrying the little parcel of food which his mother had cooked for him at dawn, and he returned late in the night, so tired that he could only eat his supper and roll up in his corner to sleep. He slept well, and was not easily disturbed. Only sometimes, when the noise in the room rose to a pitch, he woke up and opened startled eyes to scenes which, though he had seen them all his life, were still scenes of horror to him. His uncle might be reeling round the room, drunk, bedraggled, desperate, shouting:

'Let me be! Let me live!' tearing his hair and then knocking his head against the wall and whimpering in anguish. Hands clutched at him, his wife, his sister, his mother; shrill tearful voices implored him to lie down and sleep, till suddenly he broke loose and roared like a madman: 'They are eating me up!' in a voice of pain and despair. The women reeled back and it was always at that point that he began to beat his wife. He struck out at her wildly, staggering and falling like a wounded animal, sometimes hitting and sometimes missing, while she screamed on one long high-pitched note and dodged him fairly successfully. 'I will kill her!' he shouted, hitting out with both arms and tears streaming down his face. 'Kill them all!' he sobbed. Ram Kumar, woken up from his sleep, clutched his tattered blanket to his chest and stared with horrified eyes at the drunken man and the screaming women, the little flame in the kerosene lamp flickering and dying for want of oil, and the grandmother on her knees praying with uplifted hands to God to save them all.

But in the shop it was different. Here there were comfortably well-to-do customers, courteous assistants, and the proprietor who sat all day at a table in a corner of the shop. Ram Kumar had a great respect for the proprietor. He admired the way he sat poring over business letters and accounts while remaining alert to everything that went on in the shop, every now and again rapping out an order or rising himself to help satisfy a difficult customer. He was a morose man, with a clean blue shave and rimless spectacles, who never talked much and suffered from a bad stomach. If he had any personal feelings, he never showed them in the shop: an inefficient assistant was got rid of, however piteously he might plead poverty and promise reform, salaries were docked with ruthless impartiality for a damage to stock and unpunctuality. But he showed the same impartiality in recognizing merit. Ram Kumar found himself step by step promoted, first to assistant salesman, then to salesman, then to deputy head salesman and finally, after seven years, when he was twenty-two years old, to head salesman and staff manager.

He was earning good money now. His status in the family increased and, with his, his mother's. Nobody beat her now, nobody called her 'evil eye'; she was no longer the widow of her husband but the mother of her son and, as such, worthy of respect. She held her head high, bought a new sari and gave sharp answers. But she was not yet satisfied. She still wanted, as she had wanted ever since her widowhood, to be taken away by her son and set up in a home of her own. Every night she urged this on him, in cajoling whispers; every night he made no reply but turned over in his corner and went to sleep. He wanted a different domestic life, but he was always too tired, after his day at the shop, to formulate thoughts of getting it. But one day she told him she had heard of a place they could have at low rent, and after that he began to think about it. And with his mother nagging him and pleading constantly, it was easier to give way than to hold out. So they moved, he and his mother and his two younger sisters, to a ground-floor room in a tenement, and he became head of a family.

Here he had his first taste of domestic bliss. It was good to come home, late in the evening, to the quiet room which the women kept scrupulously clean, and to eat the food they had prepared for him with such love and care. They treated him, their sole support, with high respect and he, in return, took his responsibility towards them very seriously. His senior position in the shop had already given him an air of authority, a certain dignity of bearing, which he

could now afford to take home with him. He had also
borrowed his employer's somewhat sour expression of face,
and his principles were strict. Not that he was very sure of
any principles; but he knew how life should not be and
deduced from that how perhaps it should. He was sure it
should not be as he had known it in his uncle's house –
disorderly, dirty and violent; and in opposition he set up an
ideal of quiet and orderliness, of meekness and domestic
piety. To this he wished his women to adhere. He liked to
think of them quietly following their household duties,
taking in some sewing work and keeping themselves modestly
to themselves.

This last was perhaps the most important; for the tenement was full of people who led the sort of lives he wanted
to get away from. On the top floor was a Muslim insurance
clerk whose two wives were for ever quarrelling and abusing
one another, and underneath them a crippled astrologer,
who augmented his income by selling love potions and whose
dissatisfied clients frequently reported him to the police.
Next to Ram Kumar on the ground floor lived a traveller
in rugs and carpets, whose wife and daughter, left often
alone, did not conduct themselves with the decorum Ram
Kumar could have wished for in his neighbours. They stood
out in the street and laughed and joked, the mother as well
as her daughter, showing off their big breasts and healthy
cheeks. It was this family that Ram Kumar feared most, for
they made overtures of friendliness and the girl was the same
age as his sisters. He found it necessary to instruct his mother
to avoid all contact with them, which she agreed to do,
denouncing them with some fervour for loose morals and
shameless conduct.

In appearance Ram Kumar remained as he had been as
a child – small, weak and wholly unremarkable. Yet he was

getting the habit of authority: at home there was no one but he who counted, in the shop he was next only to the proprietor. He became exacting, tight with money and slightly bad-tempered. His mother forbade everything to his sisters in his name – 'Your brother will be angry' – and every evening, just before his homecoming, she as well as the two girls began to fidget about the room, tidying everything up more than was necessary. And Ram Kumar looked round, pursed his lips and thrust out his thin stomach, and felt himself master of the house.

Except when his brother was there. Vijay came to see them sometimes, and his presence had what Ram Kumar felt to be a deplorable effect on the household. For Vijay, with his silk suit, his big ring, his oiled and scented hair, at once upset that prim orderliness which Ram Kumar had imposed. The mother and sisters became flushed and excited, they hovered around Vijay, listened to his stories, tittered and fussed and were restrained only by the presence of Ram Kumar, at whom they threw frequent guilty glances. Vijay himself hardly noticed his brother. As far as he was concerned, Ram Kumar's status had not changed from the time he had been the puny and insignificant younger brother who kept out of everyone's way. Sometimes, in face of this contempt, Ram Kumar felt like asserting himself: after all, it was he who was now the head of the family and kept the mother and sisters, not Vijay who did nothing for them. Yet most of the time he was glad not to be noticed by Vijay; for he was still afraid of him.

There was to him something alien and terrible about his elder brother. He was not sure quite what work he did for the big business magnate who kept him in his retinue, but he sensed that it was something rather shady of which no one ever spoke. And that to him characterized Vijay's life alto-

gether – it was something of which one could not speak and should not even think about. Where did he live, and with whom? A shudder passed through Ram Kumar when he thought of this. He could never forget the young Muslim lady they had been told about, who sang and danced. The tunes Vijay hummed he had perhaps first heard from her, the liquor of which he smelt he had drunk with her, the ring he wore had been given by her, when he smiled like that and smoothed his hair he was thinking of her. And all this he brought with them into their room, it was behind his eyes and voice as he joked with the mother and sisters, and Ram Kumar could do nothing and say nothing and wait only for him to be gone again.

Sometimes Vijay did not go so quickly. It seemed there were periods when he was out of work or had temporarily quarrelled with his employers or simply did not feel like working, and then he hung around his brother's home, unwashed and dishevelled, sleeping with abandon, going out at nights to drink with his friends. Ram Kumar suspected that during these periods his mother supplied him with funds out of her housekeeping money, but he dared not ask and pretended not to notice. He pretended also not to notice the suppressed excitement which shone in the faces of the mother and her daughters, as if they were having a much better time than they wished him to know. But he did not wish to know and was even afraid of knowing. He went to the shop and lost himself in work. There was comfort in dressing the doll in a different outfit and hovering tender fingers over a newly-arrived stock of silk underwear.

Once, on coming home, he found the wife and daughter of the traveller in rugs and carpets in the room. They all seemed to be on the friendliest terms together. Ram Kumar's mother and his sisters looked shocked when he came in, but

Vijay and the visitors went on talking and laughing undis-
turbed. Their laughter was loud and improper, and the girl
flung back her head from a strong, healthy throat and let
Vijay look down into her bosom. Ram Kumar retired into
a corner and ate his food, while his mother whispered to
him, 'What could we do? They came to visit.' He did not
answer. When she lied, his mother's face bore a prim,
innocent expression. He hated her and hated his sisters and
hated the home he had made. The traveller's daughter
looked at him over her shoulder; she looked sly and laughing, and her little gold ear-ring shook against her plump
cheek. He knew she was laughing at him and he felt ashamed
for not being like Vijay. Yet he was angry too, because it
was he who supported the family and paid the rent of the
room in which they sat enjoying themselves, not Vijay.

After that, he often thought about the neighbours. He
thought about the plump, shameless girl and felt indignant.
He also felt it was time for him to marry off his sisters. His
mother had been telling him so for some time: 'Find someone for my girls,' she told him in the urgent whisper she
always used when she wanted something; 'it is time they
were off your hands.' Then she looked coy, gazing at him
with her head on one side and too sweet a smile on her lips:
'And after that is finished, we can start thinking of you.' She
tried to stroke his face but he turned it away. He was not
ready to think of his own marriage yet.

But he set earnestly and methodically about doing something for his sisters. He studied the matrimonial advertisement columns in the newspapers, inserted an advertisement
of his own and, after some correspondence, settled things to
everyone's satisfaction. For their dowries he had to borrow
from a moneylender at the usual rate of interest, but he
knew that with his salary he would have little difficulty in

repaying this by monthly instalments. He was pleased with himself, so was his mother. Her hints about his own marriage became more frequent, and he was more ready to listen to her.

He often saw the wife of the traveller in carpets nowadays, and her daughter. They always seemed to be outside their room when he passed in the mornings and in the evenings. The mother was very obsequious to him, she smiled humbly and inquired after his health, while the daughter hovered behind her, her head covered by her sari with a becoming, if uncharacteristic, air of modesty. Ram Kumar never looked at her, but when he passed her, he could not help thinking of the way she had glanced at him over her shoulder that night when he had seen her in his room, and her ear-ring shaking against her round, glowing cheek.

His mother began frequently mentioning these neighbours to him; at first hesitantly, but when she saw that he was inclined to listen, more fully and boldly. He had been, she said, mistaken about them. They were decent, respectable people, and the girl a jewel of a girl – modest and skilled in household duties; and moreover, the father, travelling around in a hired horse-drawn carriage with his rugs and carpets rolled up at the back, earned good money, he would be able to give a fine dowry with his only daughter. Ram Kumar listened and felt flattered. It was he who was being persuaded to take this plump pretty girl, he who was wanted for her husband, not someone else, not Vijay. Every night his mother talked to him, every morning and night he saw the girl and her mother waiting for him outside their door. His face remained sour and perhaps he even exaggerated his frown of ill-humour, to hide the strange feelings that were growing inside him. These surprised him, for he had not known that one could have such feelings.

He did not have them for long after he married her. She

soon stopped smiling for him, and his mother soon stopped
finding any virtue in her. Every day the two women
quarrelled, and the girl's mother would rush in and take
her daughter's part. When Ram Kumar came home, his
mother at once began complaining to him against his wife,
who, tossing her head and keeping a menacing silence,
glowered at him as if she dared him to say anything to her.
And he never did dare; instead he got angry with his mother,
and told her not to worry him with her women's quarrels.

He was afraid of his wife in the same way as he was afraid
of Vijay. He knew that his high position in the shop and the
important frown he wore on his face did not impress her.
When he came to her with his passion, she pushed him away
as one would push away a troublesome little animal; and
even when she let him come to her, she remained aloof and
impatient, so that afterwards he was ashamed and turned
from her with an embarrassed look on his face. He could
refuse her nothing, not because he loved her any more but
because of this fear he had of her. When she wanted money,
he had to give it, though it was always painful for him to
part with money. Sometimes he dared to protest – 'I have
given money for the household' – but it was never any use;
in the end he had to fumble in his pocket, feeling unhappy
and defeated, while she stood there with one hand on her
hip and the other insolently outstretched; and his mother,
whom he had always kept very short, looked on with
hungry, angry eyes.

When Vijay came, Ram Kumar's wife was quite different.
Then all her contempt and nonchalance dropped from her;
she smiled again as she had smiled before she was married,
dimples appeared in her fat cheeks and her sari was allowed
to slip from her bosom. And Vijay looked at her with a
knowing air, which made her laugh more and put up a hand

to caress her hair and turn herself casually to show off her hips. Ram Kumar was in the shop all day and it was easy for him there not to think about them. When he was home, he frowned in his usual way and pretended to notice nothing. He did not talk to anyone, and only his mother tried to talk to him.

It was difficult to know how his mother felt about the situation. At times she looked at Vijay with pride and gentle, wistful, motherly sighs; and at others at Ram Kumar with what was perhaps pity. She tried to talk to Ram Kumar sometimes; and strangely enough, always about his father, the long-dead printer. 'What a man,' she would say; and she sighed and smiled and wiped at a tear. She may have been talking about him in his gentle family-man aspect; yet it seemed more likely – from her tone of womanly respect and the way she looked, pityingly and comparingly, at Ram Kumar – that she was referring to him in his role of swaggering drunkard and lusty wife-beater.

What Ram Kumar still liked best in the shop, after all these years, was serving the customers. He stood waiting behind the counter, with just the right mixture of dignity and obsequiousness, his hands folded in repose at chest-level and inclining his body in a brisk, neat bow. He brought out the requisite goods almost before his customer had finished asking for them, and spread them with respectful triumph on the counter. He did not have to say 'This is the best you can buy anywhere': his quiet pride, his attitude of caressing reverence towards his goods, made that clear enough. But at the least sign of hesitation on the part of the customer, he was ready to push aside the first item and startle with something even more suitable. He reached up, reached down, swooped here and darted there to bring out more stock, snapped his fingers in the air for one of the assistants to whom he delivered terse and almost silent commands, and all this so unobtrusively, and as it were with his left hand, that his customer never for one moment felt released from his ardent attention. Sometimes, in the most respectful manner possible, he put forward a question-mark of discreet suggestion and if this met with a favourable response, began gently to guide his customer's desires. His patience and solicitude never slackened, and he remained all-absorbed till the last moment when he handed back change and cash-memo and bowed his customer off the premises with the same self-immolating grace, his hands folded, his eyes lowered, with which he had welcomed him. He felt himself alive and significant with the customers. Here he was the salesman, perfect in his role, whom no one could ignore or despise or challenge in authority.

His wife had children whom he could not care for as much as he might have done if he had been sure that they were his. Yet he provided for them, clothed them and sent them to school. He provided for everybody. His uncle, the postal inspector, died, and while his widow and smaller children went into the care of a grown-up son, the grandmother and aunt, tough old roots who lived for ever, were sent to Ram Kumar. Vijay was now often not working. He lay around in Ram Kumar's home and quarrelled with Ram Kumar's wife. He had become bloated and morose. Though he still went on his drinking bouts at night, he could not carry his liquor so well and often, when he came home, he could be heard to retch and moan right up till morning. He was mostly in a depressed mood nowadays. He sat against the wall, with his knees drawn up and his head lowered, wiping his hands in his tousle of dank hair, and grew philosophical.

'All the good things in life,' he would say, 'are like shaky teeth in the mouth, which will drop out and leave us.' Gold ring, silk suit, Muslim lady – all had gone. He was a tired, ageing man and mostly out of work. It seemed the business magnate had withdrawn his protection, and Vijay now only got work here and there from old associates. Whatever he earned, he spent, and then he wheedled Ram Kumar's wife who abused him but finally got him what he wanted from her husband. Money began to be very short in the house. Ram Kumar found he often had to turn to moneylenders, and the debts mounted and so did the interest on them. Sometimes he could not keep up with the monthly repayments and then the moneylenders came to the house and had to be cajoled.

His relations with the proprietor of the shop had never changed, in all the years he had worked there. The proprietor sat, sour and impersonal, behind his table, doing his accounts and keeping an eye on what was going on in the shop; Ram Kumar as head assistant was his right-hand man but by no means his confidant. They had no private relationship at all. Ram Kumar had shyly revealed his marriage and, later, the birth of his wife's first son, but both these items of news had been received too non-committally for him ever to venture to impart any other. He respected his employer's complete lack of interest in the lives of his employees. He understood there was a barrier as between a king and his subjects, or a guru and his disciples, and that it was right to maintain that barrier. Yet he felt closer to the proprietor than to anyone else in the world. They shared one overriding passion – their passion for the shop – and this to Ram Kumar seemed like a deep source of orderliness and virtue, of Goodness and Truth.

And yet, as he got older and things at home became more

hopeless, he began to want something further from the proprietor. He felt sometimes, as they were checking stock together or counting the day's takings, that there were other things he wished to talk about besides the business in hand. He was not sure quite what those other things might be, and yet he felt an urge to start talking from the heart; to say, perhaps, 'Sir, my wife has always been unfaithful to me,' or 'Sir, I have my mother, my grandmother, my aunt, my brother to support.' And, still more, he wanted to ask questions. There was a new why in his life that he wanted to put to someone. He could not understand how things had come to this pass: he had always worked so hard; had wanted to keep everything decent and orderly and different from what it had been in his uncle's house. Yet, in spite of his efforts, the same disorder there had been in his uncle's house, the same sense of too much and too violent a humanity, had come to swallow his own life. He felt as if everything were closing in on him – the Muslim wives fighting upstairs, the crippled astrologer and, in his own room, the monstrous shapes of his mother, his wife, his grandmother, the shrill voices, the quarrels, dirt and poverty and moneylenders who had to be cajoled. He remembered how his uncle had clutched at his head and screamed: 'They are eating me up!' and that was how he was feeling himself, devoured and eaten.

He did not know any way in which to tell this to the proprietor, so that there was nothing for him to do but push back his rising heart and continue checking stock. And afterwards, when the shop closed at night, he wandered round by himself, his lips moving slightly as he talked in imagination to the proprietor, explaining himself fully and without reservation. Often, when he got home, his wife at once began to ask him for money; and when he had to refuse her, for it frequently happened nowadays that he really had nothing, she was angry and shouted at him, while his mother listened with tightdrawn lips.

Once he tried to defend himself, he waved trembling hands in the air and cried, 'But what can I do?'

That drove her to such fury that she began to look round for something to strike him with; and she would undoubtedly have found something, if Vijay had not at this point intervened.

He turned to Ram Kumar and said, 'Why don't you ask for more money in your shop?'

But that suggestion shocked Ram Kumar; he had got to the top of the salary-scale, and the salary-scale was to him like a law of God or Nature, incontrovertible.

Vijay laughed at him and his wife shouted, 'What is it to him if we all starve!'

Vijay mocked, 'He belongs to his shop, not to us'; but after a time he stopped mocking, and his face assumed the bitter expression which nowadays was the most characteristic of him. He said, 'Yes, all your life you have slaved for the shop, and where are you now?'

Ram Kumar's wife said, 'The fool, his own family is nothing to him —'

'Keep quiet,' Vijay said, without even turning round to her; she looked sullen, but said nothing further. 'Look at both of us,' said Vijay to his brother. 'You have worked all your life and I —' here he stopped and laughed, with an echo of his old free laughter in which there was also some surprise and admiration at all the things he had done in *his* life. 'And now we are both here,' he said.

Ram Kumar listened to him, which was not something he had often done before; but now, for the first time, he felt almost a kind of response to what his brother was saying.

After that, he listened more frequently when Vijay sat on the floor in his bitter moods, running his hands through his hair and muttering against the world. 'The world sucks the juice out of us and then spits us out like an empty shrivelled skin,' said Vijay. And Ram Kumar pretended to be minding his own business, as usual, but inwardly he nodded. It was so, he knew now; he had always worked and hoped hard, but had got nothing. His attitude towards the shop and the proprietor changed, and he began to doubt whether they really represented all goodness and virtue, as he had so unquestioningly believed all these years. He still worked as hard as ever and received customers with the same grace and ceremony; but now he went about these things stiffly and hollowly and without joy, like a man who has lost his faith.

One day Vijay, when returning from one of his drinking bouts, was knocked down by a motorcycle-rickshaw. He was brought to a hospital where it took him three days to die. They covered him with a red cloth and carried him on a plank down to the Jumna. The pall bearers were Ram Kumar and several cousins and brothers-in-law. Behind them walked other male relatives and friends. Everyone chanted: 'God God, you are Truth!' Ram Kumar chanted too, but he did not believe it; he did not believe there was any God or any Truth or anything at all.

Since Vijay had no sons, it was Ram Kumar who had to feed the fire of his brother's pyre. He ladled in clarified butter and heard its sizzle and saw the flames shoot up; and it was not long before it was all finished and they could go home again. At home the women were mourning. They wailed and screamed and knocked themselves against the floor and walls to hurt themselves. Ram Kumar's wife clutched at her own throat as if she wished to strangle

herself and screamed to her dead and burnt brother-in-law:
'Stand up just once more!' The mother hit her fist against
her forehead and chanted about the feelings she had when
she was carrying Vijay, and about his childhood and beautiful manhood. The grandmother, who was very old now and
not sure who was dead, stamped her feeble feet and wrung
her hands to Heaven. Even very distant relatives, who had
hardly known Vijay, showed extravagant grief. It was what
was done at every death – what must have been done,
though Ram Kumar could not remember it, at his own
father's death, what had been done at his uncle the postal
inspector's, and what no doubt would be done at his own
death, by these women who went on for ever.

There was no spark in him to kindle him into a rebel.
And yet, as he smiled and bowed to customers, he asked
himself sometimes, why am I doing this; and he looked at
the proprietor – sitting at his table, blue-shaved, with rimless spectacles, growing every year richer and more sour –
and strange feelings rose in his heart. Meanwhile at home
money became tighter and tighter. His mother developed
some disease, which made her feet and hands swell up. She
had to be taken to doctors, and the doctors had to be paid
money, which Ram Kumar did not know how to come by.
Once she said to him, 'If I could die, son, things would be
easier for you'; she could no longer walk and sat all day on
a piece of matting, looking down in astonishment at her
purple, swollen hands that lay in her lap like dead animals.
At last Ram Kumar asked for a rise in salary. The salary-
scale had, like everything else, ceased to be sacred to him,
so it was no longer impossible for him to ask; but he expected to be refused, which he was.

His one act of rebellion was quite unpremeditated and
came as a surprise even to himself. He was dressing the doll,

changing its attire from a silk-blouse and velvet shorts to a blue dressing-gown with braidings, when he dropped it. He never quite knew whether he had done it on purpose. He remembered thinking, just before the fatal accident, that the doll's mouse-tooth grin was rather stupid; he also remembered the surge of pleasure when it went hurtling, with some violence, down from the counter. Everyone in the shop gasped and came crowding round; the proprietor rose from his table. They all stood and looked at the broken fragments and from them at Ram Kumar, who kept his eyes lowered and said nothing. He would not apologize, would not say he did not know how it could have happened. He was almost enjoying this little unexpected moment, though he would no doubt have enjoyed it more if he had not known that the cost of a new doll would be taken, month by month, out of his salary.

THE AWARD

DEV PRAKASH had already met too many such young men during the past nine years. Research students, junior lecturers, journalists whose articles seldom got into print – they seemed to be the only people who took any interest in him.

'What I am intending for my thesis,' said the young man, 'is to show how Indian writing has developed since Independence.'

'I see,' said Dev Prakash, nodding his big head with the two heavy chins and the long, greying hair sagely up and down. He had an impressive literary-lion manner, which did not betray the sense of failure and neglect he was at present feeling.

'Perhaps if you could give me some hints about present-day writings,' said the young man. 'With special reference to your own works.'

'My own works,' Dev Prakash repeated, his interest stirred. He passed a large, dimpled hand over his noble brow. 'Whatever I have written, whatever little I may have achieved, my inspiration has been, always: India.' Who repaid him by ignoring him, wasting him, passing him over. For twenty-five years he had been what he called in exile and even now that he had come home, he felt more exiled than ever. Yet he had come with such high hopes: the Tagore of today, that was what he had hoped they would call him. 'What can I tell you about my own works? They are there, to be read or to be ignored, to be loved or to be scorned.'

The young man, who had his thesis to think of, was more practical: 'If perhaps you could outline for me your position in regard to other Indian writers of today.'

Dev Prakash leaned back against a bolster. He looked up at the ceiling with a self-tolerant little smile on his lips: 'Of course, I have always been something of an odd man out.'

His sister Usha came in and said, 'We are having a dinner-party this evening.' She took no notice of the young man; like all the well-dressed, well-fed women of her set, she had horrible manners.

'Your dull, dull dinners,' said Dev Prakash with a conspiratorial smile at the young man who, however, was looking down at the papers in his lap in swollen embarrassment.

'You will be here?' Usha asked, unmoved by his comment. Most things left her unmoved; she was a tall, slow, heavy woman with a stout, faintly-moustached face out of which her magnificent dark eyes looked with boredom and discontentment.

In spite of his very sociable nature, Dev Prakash disliked these dinner-parties which his sister and her husband gave. The food was always too heavy and too much, the guests too rich and too fat; and nobody had anything at all to say. But Aruna was not free in the evening and he had nowhere else to go; so he put on a mock-martyr air and said, 'If you command me.' There was so little social life for him nowadays.

She opened his wardrobe: 'What will you wear?' She looked up and down the shelves and clicked her tongue – 'You never have anything nice.' By 'nice' she meant silk shirts and English-style jackets; whereas he was, on the one hand, too Indian and, on the other, too bohemian ever to wear anything but the national clothes of homespun cotton.

'What can you expect from a poor scribbler like me?' he replied with another smile at the young man; who, this time, responded – though wrongly, for he looked up not with an answering smile but with a look of astonishment. Dev Prakash was put out for a moment: he had forgotten that his opulent surroundings – the heavy furniture, the marble floors, the silver and the uniformed servants of his sister's household – were not really consonant with a poor scribbler. But he had always liked to refer to himself in such terms; it had been easier in London, of course, where the quaintly untidy rooms he had rented in Hampstead had not betrayed the handsome allowance that was sent to him every quarter from his share of the family business.

The young man surprisingly said, 'As junior lecturer I get a salary of only Rs.350 a month.'

Usha turned round from the wardrobe to look at him with distaste. Dev Prakash cleared his throat and ran his hand in a soft, slightly dandified movement over his shoulder-length hair.

'If I get Ph.D., I can become senior lecturer and get a salary of Rs.650 rising to Rs.900.'

Dev Prakash thought of England. Whenever he was depressed by India and Indians, he thought of England.

'That is why I am very anxious to complete this thesis and satisfy the examiners.'

He thought of interesting people with whom one could have interesting conversations. There had been the evenings in his rooms in Hampstead and other evenings in Isabel's flat in Chelsea: the cosy lamplight, the cigarettes and cups of coffee and cultured, witty people talking of literature and the arts.

Usha shut the wardrobe and sat down in an arm-chair, with her legs spread wide in front of her; she exercised her toes with the freshly-painted nails and looked at them as she did so. There was nothing studied about the way she ignored the existence of the young man; his insignificance was too real for her to have to take up an attitude about it. He realized it and suffered, keeping his eyes lowered and pressing his knees together in an unnecessary effort at further self-effacement. Dev Prakash also suffered; he had lived a long time among people who made a cult of personal relationships and consequently he kept up a social behaviour as studied and scrupulous as Usha's was the reverse. He turned to the young man and addressed him with more cordiality than he felt: 'You must stress in your thesis,' he said, smiling unnecessarily, 'that we are all of us only pioneers.'

The young man straightened the papers on his knees and continued to put the questions with which he had come prepared. 'I would like to know your opinion of your poem "My Country is a Rose in my Heart".'

Dev Prakash settled himself on his divan, supporting his cheek against his large dimpled hand, and said in a richly reminiscent mood: 'Let me tell you something of the circumstances under which it was written.'

Usha was yawning; she opened her mouth very wide and did not bother to cover it with her hand.

'I was an exile from my country. Oh perhaps, from day to day, I did not suffer acutely – I had friends, even a little recognition, I visited the theatre, there were parties – I had made some sort of a life there.' He had had many friends in England. Plump and sensuous in the tight-fitting Indian clothes he wore, with his deep dark eyes in which one could read, if one wanted to, all the sufferings of the East, he was always a success with English women; and his patriotic sentiments, which he enunciated in a low, soft

voice vibrating with feeling, woke a warm glow of indigna-
tion against oppression in all the right-thinking advanced
circles in which he moved. 'A life of exile, yes, though from
day to day, not really a bad life, not really a sad life. But all
the time,' and he straightened himself up on the divan and
his hand groped towards his heart and his eyes burned,
'there was this Ache.'

The young man, his back straight, his mouth prim, nodded and with poised pencil made a note.

'An unhealing wound in the heart,' said Dev Prakash.
He shut his eyes and quoted with passion: 'The rose is
weeping – but not tears, ah my heart! not tears.' Gooey,
Isabel had said; she was a handsome, no-nonsense woman
with an Oxford degree who wrote sensitive novels about
personal relationships. He had liked, even sometimes loved
her – but he had always been brought up short by this lack
of depth in her, this failure to feel passionately. 'Drop by
drop my rose weeps out its blood,' he said, and he still felt it,
that tear-wringing emotion that had made him write the
poem. He opened his eyes, in which there were now tears,
as often happened when he quoted his own work; he saw
that the young man too was moved. And even Usha sighed,
for she also was capable of deep feeling.

'A beautiful poem, sir,' said the young man. Dev Prakash
lowered his head in proud humility. It was true, he had had
congenial company in England, a literary life, a flattering
interest in himself and his work; while in India he had none
of these. But from time to time, as now, he was glad that
he had come home: when he felt that spontaneous love and
understanding of his work – which meant of himself, of his
soul – which he found he could get only from Indians.

Usha said, 'It is very moving.' She was materialistic, even
crude, too fond of food and clothes and the ostentation of

money; yet, more than clever, sensitive Isabel, she had this well of feeling in her to respond to the profound and the poetic.

'Sometimes people asked me,' Dev Prakash said, 'how can you, an Indian, bear to live in exile from your country? There was only one answer I could give.' His passionate eyes gazed impressively into the distance as he quoted this answer: 'It is better than to live as a slave in one's own land.' Though this was no longer an answer he could give after Independence. He had not returned until 1950, three years after Independence. He had got so used to England and his cosy, shabby rooms in Hampstead, it had been difficult to leave.

'What sort of a life can you lead there' said Usha, with some contempt. She admired many things English, such as sofa-sets, novelty lamp-stands and leather handbags, but despised the English for their food and their climate and the way they lived, and perhaps also for being English and not opulent and sensual the way she was.

'An exile's life,' said Dev Prakash with a shrug. Though really it was only after Independence that he had felt this exile status acutely. He had found then that people no longer regarded him in the same light. There had even seemed to be, though of course no one had ever spoken it, an under-mining undercurrent of why doesn't he go home? And indeed, that was a question that had also occurred to himself very frequently, and to which he had often weighed the answers.

The young man said, 'For my thesis I would like to illustrate with many quotations,' but before he had finished saying it, there was a commotion of arrival outside, a female voice called, 'He is here?' and then the door opened, and she came in – Aruna, rustling with silk, jingling with bracelets, her face glowing, her mouth smiling in expectation, eager and all on tiptoe to impart some exciting news.

'Guess what I have heard today!' she called to Dev Prakash, shining at him with pride and love. She stepped nearer and held out a plump, bejewelled hand to him: 'My great man of letters!' she said, and the way she said it, caressing him with her voice and her eyes, made the young man look down at his papers. Dev Prakash indicated him with his chin: 'This young man is writing a thesis on modern Indian writers.'

Aruna turned round to him. She had not noticed him, on her first entrance; she had better manners than Usha and did not make a habit of ignoring unimportant people. But now she made up to him for her neglect by turning her brilliant eyes and smile on him; she cried in a radiant voice, 'There you have the greatest of them all!' shooting out her short forefinger at Dev Prakash who thought, really, what is the matter with her? 'You know what I heard today?' she said to the young man, and she twinkled and smiled at him, teasing him to guess. But she could not wait any longer. She clasped her hands together and threw back her head and announced, 'He has won the Akademi award!'

Dev Prakash said, 'Who told you?' His heart was beating fast with excitement and with fears that it might not be true.

Usha and Aruna were embracing. There had been a time when Usha had taken moral objection to Aruna, but nowadays they got on very well together. They embraced with tenderness and called one another sister. 'It is a proud day,' said Aruna, and now she was dabbing a little bit in the corner of her eye.

The young man had also got up. He said, 'How happy I am to be able to be the first to give you my congratulations.'

Usha did not let him finish; she asked Aruna, 'Where did
you hear?'

'I have my little sources,' answered she, smiling slyly,
which suited her.

'It is all nonsense,' said Dev Prakash in a voice he tried to
make firm.

'So your triumph and my joy are nonsense?' she playfully
turned on him. She caressed his shoulder in a way that
forced the young man to look down again. Dev Prakash
shrugged her off; his attitude towards her was always one
of mingled love and exasperation, and at the moment, as
often happened, it was mostly exasperation. 'If you will just
tell me —' he said.

'Is it in the paper?' asked Usha. 'I haven't seen it this
morning.' She hardly ever saw it; she was not really interested in anything.

'Gokhale told me,' Aruna said.

'Gokhale!' Dev Prakash exclaimed, not in surprise but in
disgust, at which Aruna took offence. She said, 'If he
wouldn't know, then who would? He is still the Minister.'

'You are talking of Mr. Gokhale, the Government
Minister?' the young man said with awe and respect.

'Of course you would believe everything *he* says,' sneered
Dev Prakash.

'And why not?' Aruna had taken up a challenging attitude now and her nostrils were distended. She scented a
quarrel, and she had a real flair for quarrels.

'For years he had been pretending to be in love with
you . . .'

'Why pretending?' said Aruna. 'Why should he not love
me?' and she smiled in haughty triumph.

'That eunuch,' said Dev Prakash, forgetting the young
man.

She gave out a gasp of pretended horror: 'How impure your mind is.'

The young man said, 'How happy I am to be able to be the first to give you my congratulations.'

'Gokhale,' Dev Prakash snorted.

'Go then, go!' she shouted. 'See if you can find out from better information!' She crossed her arms challengingly on her bosom. They often quarrelled, she and Dev Prakash; they got terribly irritated with one another, so much so that sometimes, when they were alone together, they even pinched and slapped at one another in mutual anger. It was very different from Dev Prakash's life with cool, sensible Isabel.

'Certainly! I will!' said Dev Prakash and marched out to the telephone. Yet, with his hand already on the receiver, he knew it was not dignified for him to try and find out. Distinguished men of letters did not inquire about awards: these should be brought to them by respectful emissaries. He dialled a number, any number.

In the room Aruna smoothed herself, settled herself with dignity on the divan. 'A Minister's word is not good enough for him,' she said indignantly. But next moment she was smiling and shining again. She clapped her hands together and said, 'Usha, think, the Akademi award!' To the young man she said, 'He is such a great man, such a poet!'

'I feel honoured,' said the young man, 'to be the first —'

'He has suffered in his life for his country and his art,' said Aruna. 'Just think, for twenty-five years he lived in exile – twenty-five years, because he could not bear to be a slave!'

'The English winters are very cold,' said Usha. 'Every year he suffered from chilblains.'

'And when he came back, they did not give him the recognition he deserved,' said Aruna. 'Sometimes India doesn't know how to honour her great men. What is he doing out there by the telephone?' She jumped up and ran out to him. He was dialling another random number. She took the receiver from him and whispered, 'It is true. Really.' She pressed herself against him, soft flesh against soft flesh. 'How happy I am.'

'It is so improbable,' said Dev Prakash. 'I – the odd-man-out. . . .'

'For once they have chosen right!' Aruna cried. 'For once this honour has not gone to some poor conforming hack!' This last was his phrase: he had used it every year when the State Award had gone, as it always had gone up to now, to someone else.

In the room the young man, emboldened by the special-ness of the occasion, was making conversation with Usha. 'He is much respected in University circles,' he was saying. Usha was abstractedly scratching her thigh, which produced a rustling sound from her silk sari. 'We call him the Tagore of today,' said the young man. Usha went on scratching, but Aruna, returning hand in hand with Dev Prakash, cried, 'Yes, yes, how true!' And then she bent down and touched his feet, with the reverence of a devotee and the grace of a lover.

He raised her; he was full of dignity now. He turned to the young man and said with true humility, 'I am not worthy of the mantle of the Master.'

'There is a dinner-party tonight,' Usha told Aruna. 'You will come?'

'How I would love to! But I promised the girls . . .' Aruna, a widow, was the mother of three teen-age daughters whom she adored with fierce love. 'We shall celebrate some other day. How we shall celebrate for our hero!' And she threw him a look so ravishing, so worshipping, that his heart brimmed over, and he felt, as he sometimes did, that he had never, never, in all his not uneventful life, loved anyone as he loved her. 'There will be music, poetry, champagne to drink! The Prime Minister himself shall come to honour you, I will make him'; which no doubt she could for she had, by right of herself and her family, access and affection in many places. She turned to the young man: 'You too are invited to our party. Please come.'

The young man pressed his hands together and thanked her in a voice thick with joy and embarrassment. He had never been asked to a party before. Usha said, 'Where will you have it?' She ranged her mind over her wardrobe, could think of nothing suitable for the occasion and made up her mind to buy a new sari.

But Dev Prakash was suffering doubts again. 'It is strange that no one has seen fit to inform me,' he said, looking accusingly at Aruna.

The young man said, 'Will it be a formal party?' Like Usha, he was thinking of his wardrobe, which was highly inadequate.

'It was only decided last night,' Aruna said. 'Gokhale told me —'

'Gokhale,' said Dev Prakash with the same contempt as before.

'You are only jealous,' teased Aruna, playing coquette.

Usha said, 'Perhaps we can make a garden party.'

'What cause have I given you to be jealous?' said Aruna in a low, tender voice, bringing her face near to his. But he drew back; he was too agitated to be loving. And he was irritated with her for not taking trouble to confirm the news.

'More people can be accommodated on the lawn,' Usha said, 'than in the drawing-room.'

Aruna, always quick to follow a lead, took the loving expression off her face and assumed a sulky one instead. 'It is I, not you, who have cause,' she hinted darkly. He knew she referred to the years before they had met, the years in England. She could never hear enough about them. 'And then?' she would ask eagerly, while he, smiling in sweet reminiscence, allowed himself to be drawn out into intimate details about his life with Isabel and others. She would listen, glowing with sympathy, happy that he had had so much happiness; leading him on until he became almost maudlin with tender nostalgia; and it was always at this point that she would suddenly turn on him. 'How dare you tell me such things!' she would shout, and then she would begin to abuse him with astonishing vulgarity. A fierce quarrel followed, which always ended with her jumping out of bed and putting on her clothes with insulting haste, while she thanked God that she still had her three lovely, beautiful, innocent girls to go home to, and had no need of him.

Usha said, 'Ragho Mull's can do the catering. They are very good for garden party.'

'Nobody knows if it is true or not, and already you are arranging for the catering!' Dev Prakash, scattering his dignity, suddenly shouted at her. He felt like shouting at someone and was afraid to do so at Aruna. Indeed, now that he was angry with someone else, she was all solicitude. 'You know it is bad for you to upset yourself,' she admonished him, seating herself beside him on the divan, stroking his sleeve and making gentle clucking noises to soothe her ruffled lion.

Usha said placidly, 'Arrangements must be made in good time always.'

The young man suddenly turned to Aruna: 'If the function is to be formal, I may not be able to attend.'

'And a garden party always needs many special arrangements.'

'I may perhaps not have any right clothes to wear,' the young man explained to Aruna; and assured of her sympathy, blurted out further, 'You see, it is difficult for me to buy clothes, I have many obligations —'

'But of course it will be quite informal!' Aruna cried. Too late, however, for he had already been seized by a passion to show himself and his life to her completely: 'My mother and my widowed aunt are both living with me, I have to support them. And there is also schooling for my children – I have four children – and rents today are very high, and doctors' bills also must be paid.' He sighed. 'Life for me is often very difficult.'

Aruna sighed with him. 'Yes, life has many trials for us all.'

'I can't afford to spend anything on myself – for three years now I haven't been able to have any new clothes sewn.' He looked down ruefully at his trousers, shrunk to the ankle, at his shirt, very clean but frayed at collar and cuffs. 'It will be difficult for me to come to your party like this – I shall feel ashamed before your other guests.'

Dev Prakash, who had been in England in the angry 'thirties and the democratic 'forties and had absorbed all the best ideas, drew himself up to his full poet's dignity. His chest swelled, his large head with the long hair and plump chin and cheeks became almost leonine. 'My friend,' he said in a deep, sonorous, commanding voice. 'The simpleness of your attire is in our eyes not a drawback but even a recommendation.' He left a pause for emphasis, but Aruna ruined it for him: 'In our India,' she cried, 'it is only the simple man we admire, he who wants nothing from the world! Look at our Mahatma, what did he wear? One loincloth, finished – and yet, was there ever a greater man?'

'I was going to say,' said Dev Prakash with dignified patience, 'that in spite of the example of the Mahatma and other great spirits, we Indians lay too great a value on mere outward appearance.'

Usha, for whom this conversation held no interest, was staring in front of her with heavy eyes. She wriggled a toe and felt dissatisfaction with her life, though she could not have said what it was she wanted in place of what she had.

'We are,' said Dev Prakash, placing his hands on his knees, tight and plump in their white leggings, 'materialistic in the worst sense of the word.' Outside the telephone was ringing. Dev Prakash raised his hands from his knees and became eloquent: 'What need for me but the garden of the spirit in which to walk with my Beloved,' he quoted from his own works.

'How beautiful,' said Aruna.

A servant came in to call Dev Prakash to the telephone. When he had gone, Aruna said with an admiring sigh, 'He is such a poet, such a fine soul, he sees everything different from ordinary people.'

The young man told her, 'I am very anxious to better my position.'

'It is our duty in life to strive,' she sympathized.

'If I complete my thesis and am successful in obtaining the Ph.D. degree, I can apply for the position of senior lecturer.'

Usha, thinking back to the new sari she contemplated buying, said, 'There is a good selection of Benares silks in the shops.' Her voice was languid and yawning, for though she regarded the acquisition of new things as a necessity, she had no real passion for it.

'As senior lecturer I can earn higher salary,' the young man said.

Dev Prakash stood framed in the doorway; his face glowed

from out of his prophet-like hair. 'It seems your information was correct,' he told Aruna in a voice he tried to keep steady.

She rose to her feet. The young man too rose. They stood looking at Dev Prakash. 'The Akademi award,' Aruna said in a breathless, happy voice.

'But you knew,' Usha pointed out.

'Of course I knew!' she cried. She flew to the cupboard under his desk in which Dev Prakash kept a bottle of rum and glasses for visitors who cared for that kind of thing. She was inexpert with the bottle, but she managed to pour four drinks. 'At least some little celebration there must be!'

The young man tried to excuse himself – he never touched spirits – but she insisted. So they all four stood drinking the rum none of them liked. Dev Prakash was grave and contained, vibrating with fulfilment. There had been gayer parties in England, wittier people, better drink which was drunk with enjoyment; but never had he felt there this oneness, this love, this union of spirit.

The young man said, 'How auspicious it is for me that I am here today.'

'You also will be successful,' Aruna said. She put down her glass and shed glad tears: 'What happiness, such happiness,' she said, loving everyone.

THE WIDOW

Durga lived downstairs in the house she owned. There was a small central courtyard and many little rooms opening out from it. All her husband's relatives, and her own, wanted to come and live with her; they saw that it would be very comfortable, and anyway, why pay rent elsewhere when there was that whole house? But she resisted them all. She wouldn't even allow them to live in the upstairs part, but let it out to strangers and took rent and was a landlady. She had learnt a lot since she had become a widow and a property-owner. No one, not even her elder relatives, could talk her into anything.

Her husband would have been pleased to see her like that. He hated relatives anyway, on principle: and he hated weak women who let themselves be managed and talked into things. That was what he had always taught her: stand on your own, have a mind, be strong. And he had left her everything so that she could be. When he had drafted his will, he had cackled with delight, thinking of all his relatives and how angry they would be. His one anxiety had been that she would not be able to stand up to them and that she would give everything over into their hands; so that his last energies had been poured into training her, teaching her, making her strong.

She had grown fond of him in those last years – so much so that, if it hadn't been for the money and independent position with which he left her, she would have been sad at losing him. That was a great change from what she had felt at the beginning of her marriage when, God forgive her, she had prayed every day for him to die. As she had pointed out in her prayers, he was old and she was young; it was not right. She had hated everyone in those days – not only her husband, but her family too, who had married her to him. She would not speak to anyone. All day she sat in a little room, unbathed, unkempt, like a woman in mourning. The servant left food for her on a tray and tried to coax her to eat, but she wouldn't—not till she was very hungry indeed and then she ate grudgingly, cursing each mouthful for keeping her alive.

But the old man was kind to her. He was a strange old man. He did not seem to expect anything of her at all, except only that she should be there in his house. Sometimes he brought saris and bangles for her, and though at first she pretended she did not want them, afterwards she was pleased and tried them on and admired herself. She often wondered why he should be so kind to her. He wasn't to anyone else. In fact, he was known as a mean, spiteful old man, who had made his money (in grain) unscrupulously, pressed his creditors hard and maliciously refused to support his needy relatives. But with her he was always gentle and even generous, and after a while they got on very well together.

So when he was dead, she almost missed him, and it was only when she reminded herself of other things about him – his old-man smell, and his dried legs, when she had massaged them, with the useless rag of manhood flopping against the thigh – that she realized it was better he was gone. She was, after all, still young and healthy and hearty, and now with the money and property he had left her, she could lead the life she was entitled to. She kept two servants, got up when she wanted and went to sleep when she wanted; she ate everything she liked and as much as she liked; when she felt like going out, she hired a tonga – and not just any tonga, but always a spruce one with shining red-leather seats and a well-groomed horse wearing jingling bells, so that people looked round at her as she was driven smartly through the streets.

It was a good life, and she grew plump and smooth with it. Nor did she lack for company: her own family and her husband's were always hovering around her and, now that she had them in the proper frame of mind, she quite enjoyed entertaining them. It had taken her some time to get them into that proper frame of mind. For in the beginning, when her husband had just died, they had taken it for granted that she was to be treated as the widow – that is, the cursed one who had committed the sin of outliving her husband and was consequently to be numbered among the outcasts. They had wanted – yes, indeed they had – to strip her of her silken coloured clothes and of her golden ornaments. The more orthodox among them had even wanted to shave her head, to reduce her diet to stale bread and lentils and deprive her from ever again tasting the sweet things of life: to condemn her, in fact, to that perpetual mourning, perpetual expiation, which was the proper lot of widows. That was how they saw it and how their forefathers had always seen it; but not how she saw it at all.

There had been a struggle, of course, but not one of which the outcome was long in doubt. And now it was accepted that she should be mistress of what was hers and rule her household and wear her fine clothes and eat her fine foods: and out of her abundance she would toss crumbs to them, let them sit in her house and talk with them when she felt like talking, listen to their importunities for money and sometimes even perhaps – not out of pity or affection,

but just as the whim took her – do them little favours and
be praised and thanked for it. She was queen, and they knew
it.

But even a queen's life does not bring perfect satisfaction
always, and there were days and even weeks at a time when
she felt she had not been dealt with as she had a right to
expect. She could never say exactly what had been left out,
but only that something *had* been left out and that somehow,
somewhere, she had been short-changed. And when this
realization came over her, then she fell into a black mood
and ate and slept more than ever – not for pleasure, but
compulsively, sunk in sloth and greed because soft beds and
foods were all that life had given to her. At such times she
turned her relatives away from her house, and those who
nevertheless wheedled their way in had to sit respectfully
silent round her bed while she heaved and groaned like a
sick woman.

There was one old aunt, known by everyone as Bhuaji,
who always managed to wheedle her way in, whatever
Durga's mood. She was a tough, shrewd old woman, small
and frail in appearance and with a cast in one eye which
made it seem as if she was constantly peeping round the next
corner to see what advantage lay there. When Durga's
black mood was on her, it was Bhuaji who presided at the
bedside, saw to it that the others kept suitably mournful
faces and, at every groan of Durga's, fell into loud exclama-
tions of pity at her sufferings. When Durga finally got tired
of all these faces gathered round her and, turning her back
on them, told them to go away and never come back to be
a torture and a burden on her, then it was again Bhuaji who
saw to it that they left in haste and good order and suitably
on compassionate tiptoe; and after locking the door behind them all, she would come back to sit with Durga

and encourage her not only to groan but to weep as well and begin to unburden herself.

Only what was there of which she could unburden herself, much as, under Bhuaji's sympathetic encouragement, she longed to do so? She brought out broken sentences, broken complaints and accusations, but there was nothing she could quite lay her finger on. Bhuaji, always eager and ready to comfort with the right words, tried to lay it on for her, pointing out how cruelly fate had dealt with her in depriving her of what was every woman's right – namely, a husband and children. But no, no, Durga would cry, that was not it, that was not what she wanted: and she looked scornful, thinking of those women who did have husbands and children, her sisters and her cousins, thin shabby over-worked and overburdened, was there anything to envy in their lot? On the contrary, it was they who should and did envy Durga – she could read it in their eyes when they looked at her, who was so smooth and well-fed and had everything that they could never even dream for.

Then gradually, Bhuaji began to talk to her of God. Durga knew about God, of course. One had to worship Him in the temple and also perform certain rites such as bathing in the river when there was an eclipse and give food to the holy men and observe fast-days. One did all these things so that no harm would befall, and everybody did them and had always done them: that was God. But Bhuaji talked differently. She talked about Him as if He were a person whom one could get to know, like someone who would come and visit in the house and sit and talk and drink tea. She spoke of Him mostly as Krishna, sometimes as the baby Krishna and sometimes as the lover Krishna. She had many stories to tell about Krishna, all the old stories which Durga knew well, for she had heard them since she was a child; but

Bhuaji told them as if they were new and had happened
only yesterday and in the neighbourhood. And Durga sat
up on her bed and laughed : 'No, really, he did that?' 'Yes
yes, really – he stole the butter and licked it with his fingers
and he teased the young girls and pulled their hair and kissed
them – oh, he was such a naughty boy!' And Durga rocked
herself to and fro with her hands clasped before her face,
laughing in delight – 'How naughty!' she cried. 'What a
bad bad boy, bless his heart!'

But when they came to the lover Krishna, then she sat
quite still and looked very attentive, with her mouth a little
open and her eyes fixed on Bhuaji's face. She didn't say
much, just listened ; only sometimes she would ask in a low
voice, 'He was very handsome?' 'Oh very,' said Bhuaji, and
she described him all over again – lotus eyes and brows like
strung bows and a throat like a conch. Durga couldn't form
much of a picture from that, but never mind, she made her
own, formed it secretly in her mind as she sat there listening
to Bhuaji, and grew more and more thoughtful, more and
more silent.

Bhuaji went on to tell her about Krishna's devotees and
the rich rewards granted to those whose hearts were open to
receive him. As Durga avidly listened, she narrated the life
of Maya Devi, who had retired from the world and built
herself a little hut on the banks of the Ganges : there to pass
her days with the baby Krishna, whom she had made her
child and to whom she talked all day as to a real child, and
played with him and cooked for him, bathed his image and
dressed it and put it to sleep at night and woke it up with a
kiss in the morning. And then there was Pushpa Devi, for
whom so many advantageous offers had come but who
rejected them all because she said she was wedded already,
to Krishna, and he alone was her lord and her lover ; she

lived with him in spirit, and sometimes in the nights her family could hear her screams of joy as she lay with him in their marital rite and gave him her soul.

Durga bought two little brass images of Krishna – one of him playing the flute, the other as a baby crawling on all fours. She gave them special prominence on her little prayer-table and paid her devotions to him many times a day, always waiting for him to come alive for her and be all that Bhuaji promised he would be. Sometimes – when she was alone at night or lay on her bed in the hot, silent afternoons, her thoughts dwelling on Krishna – she felt strange new stirrings within her which were almost like illness, with a tugging in the bowels and a melting in the thighs. And she trembled and wondered whether this was Krishna descending on her, as Bhuaji promised he would, showing her his passion, creeping into her – ah! great God that he was – like a child or a lover, into her womb and into her breasts.

She became dreamy and withdrawn, so that her relatives, quick to note this change, felt freer to come and go as they pleased and sit around in her house and drink tea with a lot of milk and sugar in it. Bhuaji, indeed, was there almost all the time. She had even brought a bundle of clothes and often stayed all day and all night, only scurrying off to have a quick look at her own household, with her own old husband in it, and coming back within the hour. Durga suspected that, on these home-excursions of hers, Bhuaji went well provided with little stocks of rice and lentils and whatever other provisions she could filch from the kitchen store. But Durga hardly cared and was, at any rate, in no frame of mind to make a scene. And when they asked for money, Bhuaji or the other relatives, as often as not she gave – quite absentmindedly, taking out her keys to unlock the steel almira in which she kept her cashbox, while they eagerly, greedily, watched her.

At such moments she often thought of her husband and of what he would say if he could see her being so yielding with these relatives. She could almost imagine him getting angry – hear his shrill old man's voice and see him shaking his fist so that the sleeve of his kurta flapped and showed his plucked, dried arm trembling inside. But she did not care for his anger; it was her life, her money, she sullenly answered him, and she could let herself be exploited if she wished. Why should he, a dead old man, dictate his wishes to her, who was alive and healthy and a devotee of Krishna's? She found herself thinking of her husband with dislike. It was as if she bore him some grudge, though she did not know what for.

The relatives sat in the house and got bolder and bolder, until they were giving their own orders to the servants and complaining about the quality of the tea.

It was about this time that the tenants who had rented the place upstairs gave notice – an event which brought great excitement into the lives of the relatives, who spent many happy hours apportioning the vacant flat out among themselves (Bhuaji, of course, was going to move her old husband into one room, and she left the others to fight for the remaining space). But here suddenly Durga showed herself quite firm again: tenants meant rent, and she had no intentions, not even to spite her husband, of sacrificing a regular monthly income. So only a few days after the old tenants moved out, and the relatives were still hotly disputing among themselves as to how the place was to be apportioned, a new family of tenants moved in, consisting of one Mr. Puri (a municipal tax inspector) with his wife, two daughters and a son. Their belongings were carried upstairs to loud, remonstrative cries from the relatives; to which Durga turned a deaf ear — even to the plaints of Bhuaji, who had already brought her old husband and her household chattels along and now had to take them back again.

Durga had been worshipping her two images for so long now, but nothing of what Bhuaji had promised seemed to be happening to them. And less and less was happening to her. She tried so hard, lying on her bed and thinking of Krishna and straining to reproduce that wave of love she had experienced; but it did not return or, if it did, came only as a weak echo of what it had been. She was unsatisfied and felt that much had been promised and little given. Once, after she had prayed for a long time before the two images, she turned away and suddenly kicked at the leg of a chair and hurt her toe. And sometimes, in the middle of doing something — sorting the laundry or folding a sari — she would suddenly throw it aside with an impatient gesture and walk away frowning.

She spent a lot of time sitting on a string-cot in her courtyard, not doing anything nor thinking anything in particular, just sitting there, feeling heavy and too fat and wondering what there was in life that one should go on living it. When her relatives came to visit her, she as often as not told them to go away, even Bhuaji; she did not feel like talking or listening to any of them. But now there was a new person to stake a claim to her attention. The courtyard was overlooked by a veranda which ran the length of the flat upstairs. On this veranda Mrs. Puri, her new tenant, would frequently appear, leaning her arms on the balustrade and shouting down in friendly conversation. Durga did not encourage her and answered as dryly as politeness permitted; but Mrs. Puri was a friendly woman and persisted, appearing twice and three times a day to comment to Durga on the state of the weather. After a while she even began to exercise the prerogative of a neighbour and to ask for little loans – one day she had run out of lentils, a second out of flour, a third out of sugar. In return, when she cooked a special dish or made pickle, she would send some down for Durga, thus establishing a neighbourly traffic which Durga had not wished for but was too lethargic to discourage.

Then one day Mrs. Puri sent some ginger pickle down with her son. He appeared hesitantly in the courtyard, holding his glass jar carefully between two hands. Durga was lying drowsily on her cot; her eyes were shut and perhaps she was even half asleep. The boy stood and looked down at her, not knowing what to do, lightly coughing to draw her attention. Her eyes opened and stared up at him. He was perhaps seventeen years old, a boy with large black eyes and broad shoulders and cheeks already dark with growth. Durga lay and stared up at him, seeing nothing but his young face looming above her. He looked back at her, uncertain, tried to smile, and blushed. Then at last she sat up and adjusted the sari which had slipped down from her breasts. His eyes modestly lowered, he held the jar of pickle out to her as if in appeal.

'Your Mother sent?'

He nodded briefly and, placing the jar on the floor by her cot, turned to go rather quickly. Just as he was about to disappear through the door leading out from the courtyard, she called him back, and he stopped and stood facing her, waiting. It was some time before she spoke, and then all she could think to say was 'Please thank your mother.' He disappeared before she could call him back again.

Durga had become rather slovenly in her habits lately, but that evening she dressed herself up in one of her better saris and went to call on Mrs. Puri upstairs. A visit from the landlady was considered of some importance, so Mrs. Puri, who had been soaking raw mangoes, left this work, wiped her hands on the end of her sari and settled Durga in the sitting-room. The sitting-room was not very grand, it had only a cane-table in it and some cane-stools and a few cheap bazaar pictures on the whitewashed walls. Durga sat in the only chair in the room, a velvet arm-chair which had the velvet rubbed bare in many places and smelt of old damp clothes.

Mrs. Puri's two daughters sat on the floor, stitching a quilt together out of many old pieces. They were plain girls with heavy features and bad complexions. Mr. Puri evidently was out – and his wife soon dwelt on that subject: every night, she said, he was sitting at some friend's house, goodness knows what they did, sitting like that, what could they have so much to talk about? And wasting money in smoking cigarettes and chewing betel, while she sat at home with her daughters, poor girls, and wasn't it high time good husbands were found for them? But what did Mr. Puri care – he had thought only for his own enjoyment, his family was nothing to him. And Govind the same. . . .

'Govind?'

'My son. He too – only cinema for him and laughing with friends.'

She had much to complain about and evidently did not often have someone whom she could complain to; so she made the most of Durga. The two plain daughters listened placidly, stitching their quilt; only when their mother referred to the urgent necessity of finding husbands for them – as she did at frequent intervals and as a sort of capping couplet to each particular complaint – did they begin to wriggle and exchange sly glances and titter behind their hands.

It took Durga some time before she could disengage herself; and when she finally did, Mrs. Puri accompanied her to the stairs, carrying her burden of complaint right over into her farewell and even pursuing Durga with it as she picked her way down the steep, narrow stone stairs. And just as she had reached the bottom of them, Govind appeared to walk up them, and his mother shouted down to him, 'Is this a time to come home for your meal?'

Durga passed him in the very tight space between the doorway and the first step. She was so close to him that she could feel his warmth and hear his breath. Mrs. Puri shouted down the stairs: 'Running here and there all day like a loafer!' Durga could see his eyes gleaming in the dark and he could see hers; for a moment they looked at each other. Durga said in a low voice, 'Your mother is angry with you,' and then he was already half-way up the stairs.

Later, slowly unwinding herself from her sari and staring at herself in the mirror as she did so, she thought about her husband. And again, and stronger than ever, she had that feeling of dislike against him, that grudge against the useless dead old man. It was eighteen or nineteen years now since they had married her to him: and if he had been capable, wouldn't she have had a son like Govind now, a strong, healthy, handsome boy with big shoulders and his beard just growing? She smiled at the thought, full of tenderness, and forgetting her husband, thought instead how it would be if Govind were her son. She would not treat him like his mother did – would never reproach him, shout at him down the stairs – but, on the contrary, encourage him in all his pleasures so that, first thing when he came home, he would

call to her – 'Mama!' – and they would sit together affectionately, more like brother and sister, or even two friends,
than like mother and son, while he told her everything that
had happened to him during the day.

She stepped closer to the mirror – her sari lying carelessly
where it had fallen round her feet – and looked at herself,
drawing her hand over her skin. Yes, she was still soft and
smooth and who could see the tiny little lines, no more than
shadows, that lay round her eyes and the corners of her
mouth? And how fine her eyes still were, how large and
black and how they shone. And her hair too – she unwound
it from its pins and it dropped down slowly, heavy and black
and sleek with oil, and not one grey hair in it.

As she stood there, looking at herself in nothing but her
short blouse and her waist-petticoat, with her hair down,
suddenly another image appeared behind her in the mirror:
an old woman, grey and shabby and squinting and with an
ingratiating smile on her face. 'I am not disturbing?' Bhuaji
said.

Durga bent down to pick up her sari. She began to fold it,
but Bhuaji took it from her and did it far more deftly, the
tip of her tongue eagerly protruding from her mouth.

'Why did you come?' Durga said, watching her. Bhuaji
made no reply, but went on folding the sari, and when she
had finished, she smoothed it ostentatiously from both sides.
Durga lay down on the bed. As a matter of fact, she found
she was quite glad that Bhuaji had come to see her.

She asked, 'How long is it since they married me?'

'Let me see,' Bhuaji said. She squatted by the side of the
bed and began to massage Durga's legs. 'Is it fifteen years,
sixteen . . .'

'No, eighteen.'

Bhuaji nodded in agreement, her lips mumbling as she

worked something out in her head, her hands still skilfully massaging.

'Eighteen years,' Durga said reflectively. 'I could have been—'

'Yes, a grandmother by now,' said Bhuaji, smiling widely with all her empty gums.

Durga suddenly pushed those soothing massaging hands away and sat upright. 'Leave me alone! Why do you come here, who called you?'

Instead of sitting in her courtyard, Durga was now often to be found pacing up and down by the door which led to the staircase. When Govind came down, she always had a word for him. At first he was shy with her and left her as quickly as possible; sometimes he waited for her to go away before he came down or went up. But she was patient with him. She understood and even sympathized with his shyness: he was young, awkward perhaps like a child, and didn't know how much good she meant him. But she persevered; she would ask him questions like: 'You go often to the cinema?' or 'What are you studying?' to prove to him how interested she was in him, interested like a mother or a favourite aunt, and ready to talk on any topic with him.

And slowly he responded. Instead of dashing away, he began to stand still at the bottom of the steps and to answer her questions; at first in monosyllables but soon, when his interest was stirred, at greater length; and finally at such great length that it seemed pointless to go on standing there in that dark cramped space when he could go into her house and sit there with her and drink almond sherbet. He kept on talking and told her everything: who were his friends, who his favourite film stars, his ambition to go abroad, to become an aircraft engineer. She listened and watched him while he spoke; she watched and watched him, her eyes

fixed on his face. She became very familiar with his face,
yet always it was new to her. When he smiled, two little
creases appeared in his cheeks. His teeth were large and
white, his hair sprang from a point on his forehead. Everything about him was young and fresh and strong – even his
smell, which was that of a young animal full of sap and
sperm.

She loved to do little things for him. At first only to ply
him with almond sherbet and sweetmeats, of which he could
take great quantities; later to give him money – beginning
with small amounts, a rupee here and there, but then going
on to five- and even ten-rupee notes. He wanted money so
badly and his parents gave him so little. It was wrong to
keep a boy short of money when he needed a lot: for treating
his friends, for his surreptitious cigarettes, for tee-shirts and
jeans such as he saw other boys wearing.

It became so that he got into the habit of asking her for
whatever he wanted. How could she refuse? On the contrary, she was glad and proud to give – if only to see the
look of happiness on his face, his eyes shining at the thought
of what he was going to buy, his smile which brought little
creases into his cheeks. At such moments she was warm and
sick with mother's love, she longed to cradle his head and
stroke his hair. He was her son, her child.

That was exactly what his mother told her: 'He is your
son also, your child.' Mrs. Puri was glad to see Durga take
such an interest in the boy. She taught him to say thank you
for everything that Durga gave him and to call her auntie.
She made pickle very often and sent it down in jars. She
also came down herself and talked to Durga for hours on
end about her family problems. So much was needed, and
where was it all to come from? Mr. Puri's salary was small –
175 rupees a month plus dearness allowance – and he spent

a lot on betel and cigarettes and other pleasures. And what was to become of her poor children? Such good children they were, as anyone who took an interest in them was bound to find out. They needed a helping hand in life, that was all. Her boy, and her two girls who ought to have been married a year ago. She sent the girls down quite often, but Durga always sent them quickly back up again.

Towards the beginning of each month, when the rent was due, Govind came down every day with pickle and after a while Mrs. Puri would follow him. Dabbing with her sari in the corner of her eye, she would give an exact account of her monthly expenditure, what were her debts and what she had in hand, so that Durga could see for herself how impossible it was to impose any demand for rent on such an overburdened budget. And though Durga at first tried to ignore these plaints, this became more and more difficult, and in the end she always had to say that she would not mind waiting a few days longer. After which Mrs. Puri dried her eyes and the subject of rent was not mentioned again between them till the first week of the following month, when the whole procedure was repeated. In this way several months' rent accumulated – a fact which, had it been brought to their notice, would have surprised Durga's previous tenants who had not found her by any means so lenient a landlady.

The relatives were much alarmed at this growing friendship with the Puris, which seemed to them both ominous and unnatural. What need had Durga to befriend strangers when there were all her own relatives, to whom she was bound in blood and duty? They became very indignant with her, but had to keep a check on their tongues; for Durga was short-tempered with them these days and, if they touched on subjects or showed moods not to her liking, was quicker than ever to show them the door. But something obviously had to be said and it was Bhuaji who took it upon herself to say it.

She began by praising Govind. A good boy, she said, that she could see at a glance, respectful and well-mannered, just the sort of boy whom one ought to encourage and help on in life. She had nothing at all against Govind. But his mother now, and his sisters – Bhuaji, looking sideways at Durga, sadly shook her head. Alas, she knew women like that only too well, she had come across too many of them to be taken in by their soft speech. Greedy and shameless, that was what they were, self-seeking and unscrupulous, with their one aim to fasten upon and wring whatever advantage they could out of noble-hearted people like Durga. It was they, said Bhuaji, coming closer and whispering behind her hand as if afraid Mrs. Puri would hear from upstairs, who incited the boy to come down and ask for money and new clothes – just as a feeler and to see how far they could go. Let Durga wait and in a short time she would see: saris they would ask for, not ten-rupee notes but hundred-rupee ones, household furniture, a radio, a costly carpet; and they would not rest till they had possessed themselves not only of the upstairs part of the house but of the downstairs part as well.

Just then Govind passed the door and Durga called out to him. When he came, she asked him, 'Where are you going?' and then she stroked the shirt he was wearing, saying, 'I think it is time you had another new bush-shirt.'

'A silk one,' he said, which made Durga smile and reply in a soft, promising voice, 'We will see,' while poor Bhuaji stood by and could say nothing, only squint and painfully smile.

One day Bhuaji went upstairs. She said to Mrs. Puri: 'Don't let your boy go downstairs so much. She is a healthy

woman, and young in her thoughts.' Mrs. Puri chose to take
offence: she said her boy was a good boy, and Durga was
like another mother to him. Bhuaji squinted and laid her
finger by the side of her nose, as one who could tell more if
she but chose. This made Mrs. Puri very angry and she
began to shout about how much evil thought there was in
the world today so that even pure actions were misinter-
preted and made impure. Her two daughters, though they
did not know what it was all about, also looked indignant.
Mrs. Puri said she was proud of her son's friendship with
Durga. It showed he was better than all those other boys
who thought of nothing but their own pleasures and never
cared to listen to the wisdom they could learn from their
elders. And she looked from her veranda down into the
courtyard, where Govind sat with Durga and was trying
to persuade her to buy him a motor-scooter. Bhuaji also
looked down, and she bit her lip so that no angry word
could escape her.

Durga loved to have Govind sitting with her like that. She
had no intention of buying him a motor-scooter, which
would take more money than she cared to disburse, but she
loved to hear him talk about it. His eyes gleamed and his
hair tumbled into his face as he told her about the beautiful
motor-scooter possessed by his friend Ram, which had many
shiny fittings and a seat at the back on which he gave rides
to his friends. He leaned forward and came closer in his
eagerness to impart his passion to her. He was completely
carried away – 'It does forty miles per hour, as good as any
motor-car!' – and looked splendid, full of strength and
energy. Durga laid her hand on his knee and he didn't
notice. 'I have something for you inside,' she said in a low,
hoarse voice.

He followed her into the room and stood behind her while

she fumbled with her keys at her steel almira. Her hand was shaking rather, so that she could not turn the key easily. When she did, she took something from under a pile of clothes and held it out to him. 'For you,' she said. It was a penknife. He was disappointed, he lowered his eyes and said, 'It is nice,' in a sullen, indifferent voice. But then at once he looked up again and he wetted his lips with his tongue and said, 'Only 1,200 rupees, just slightly used, it is a chance in a million' – looking past her into the almira where he knew there was a little safe in which she kept her cash. But already she was locking it and fastening the key back to the string at her waist. He suddenly reached out and held her hand with the key in it – '1,200 rupees,' he said in a whisper as low and hoarse as hers had been before. And when she felt him so close to her, so eager, so young, so passionate, and his hand actually holding hers, she shivered all over her body and her heart leaped up in her and next thing she was sobbing. 'If you knew,' she cried, 'how empty my life has been, how lonely!' and the tears flowed down her face. He let go her hand and stepped backwards, and then backwards again as she followed him; till he was brought up short by her bed which he could feel pressing against the back of his knees, as he stood, pinned, between it and her.

She was talking fast, about how alone she was and there was no one to care for. Yet she was young still, she told him – she invited him to look, look down into her face, wasn't it a young face still, and full and plump? And the rest of her too, all full and plump, and when she was dressed nicely in one of her best saris with a low-cut blouse, then who would know that she wasn't a young girl or at least a young woman in the very prime of her life? And she was good too, generous and good and ready to do everything, give everything for those she loved. Only who was there whom she could love

with all the fervour of which her heart was capable? In her
excitement she pushed against him so that he fell backwards
and sat down abruptly on her bed. At once she was sitting
next to him, very close, her hand on his – if he knew, she
said, what store of love there was in her, ready and bursting
and brimming in her! Then it was his turn to cry, he said,
'I want a motor-scooter, that's all,' in a hurt grieved voice,
trembling with tears like a child's.

That was the last time he came down to see her. Afterwards he would hardly talk to her at all – even when she
lay in wait for him by the stairs, he would brush hurriedly
past her, silent and with averted face. Once she called after
him, 'Come in, we will talk about the motor-scooter!' but
all she got by way of reply was, 'It is sold already,' tossed
over his shoulder as he ran upstairs. She was in despair and
wept often and bitterly; there was a pain right in her heart,
such as she had never experienced before. She longed to die
and yet at the same time she felt herself most burningly
alive. She visited Mrs. Puri several times and stayed for
some hours; during which Mrs. Puri, as usual, talked a lot,
and in the usual strain, and kept pointing out how her
children were Durga's too, while the two daughters simpered. Evidently she knew nothing of what had happened,
and assumed that everything was as it had been.

But, so Durga soon learned, Mrs. Puri knew very well that
everything was not as it had been. Not only did she know,
but it was she herself who had brought about the change.
It was she who, out of evil and spite, had stopped Govind
from coming downstairs and had forbidden him ever to
speak to Durga again. All this Durga learned from Bhuaji,
one hot afternoon as she lay tossing on her bed, alternately

talking, weeping and falling into silent fits of despair. She had no more secrets from Bhuaji. She needed someone before whom she could unburden herself, and who more fit for that purpose than the ever available, ever sympathetic Bhuaji? So she lay on her bed and cried: 'A son, that is all I want, a son!' And Bhuaji was soothing and understood perfectly. Of course Durga wanted a son; it was only natural, for had not God set maternal feelings to flow sweetly in every woman's breast? And now, said Bhuaji angrily, to have that God-given flow stopped in its course by the machinations of a mean-hearted, jealous, selfish woman — and so it all came out. It was a revelation to Durga. Her tears ceased and she sat up on her bed. She imagined Govind suffering under the restraint laid upon him and yearning for Durga and all her kindness as bitterly as she yearned for him. There was sorrow upstairs and sorrow downstairs. She sat very upright on the bed. After a while she turned her face towards Bhuaji, and her lips were tight and her eyes flashed. She said, 'We will see whose son he is.'

She waited for him by the stairs. He came late that night, but still she went on waiting. She was patient and almost calm. She could hear sounds from upstairs — a clatter of buckets, water running, Mrs. Puri scolding her daughters. At the sound of that voice, hatred swelled in Durga so that she was tempted to leave her post and run upstairs to confront her enemy. But she checked herself and remained standing downstairs, calm and resolute and waiting. She would not be angry. This was not the time for anger.

She heard him before she saw him. He was humming a little tune to himself. Probably he had been to see a film with friends and now he was singing a lyric from it. He sounded gay and light-hearted. She peeped out from the dark doorway and saw him clearly just under the lamp-post

outside the house. He was wearing an orange tee-shirt
which she had given him and which clung closely to him so
that all his broad chest and his nipples were outlined; his
black jeans too fitted tight as a glove over his plump young
buttocks. She edged herself as close as she could against the
wall. When he entered the doorway, she whispered his
name. He stopped singing at once. She talked fast, in a low
urgent voice: 'Come with me — what do your parents ever
do for you?'

He shuffled his feet and looked down at them in the dark.

'With me you will have everything — a motor-scooter—'

'It is sold.'

'A new one, a brand-new one! And also you can study to
be an aircraft engineer, anything you wish —'

'Is that you, son?' Mrs. Puri called from upstairs.

Durga held fast to his arm: 'Don't answer,' she whispered.

'Govind! Is that boy come home at last?' And the two
plain sisters echoed: 'Govind!'

'I can do so much for you,' Durga whispered. 'And what
can they do?'

'Coming, Ma!' he called.

'Everything I have is for you—'

'You and your father both the same! All night we have to
wait for you to come and eat your food!'

Durga said, 'I have no one, no one.' She was stroking his
arm which was smooth and muscular and matted with long
silky hair.

Mrs. Puri appeared at the top of the stairs: 'Just let me
catch that boy, I will twist his ears for him!'

'You hear her, how she speaks to you?' whispered Durga
with a flicker of triumph. But Govind wrenched his arm
free and bounded up the stairs towards his mother.

It did not take Bhuaji long after that to persuade Durga to get rid of her tenants. There were all those months of rent unpaid, and besides, who wanted such evil-natured people in the house? Bhuaji's son-in-law had connexions with the police, and it was soon arranged: a constable stood downstairs while the Puri's belongings – the velvet arm-chair, an earthenware water-pot, two weeping daughters carrying bedding – slowly descended. Durga did not see them. She was sitting inside before the little prayer-table on which stood her two Krishnas. She was unbathed and in an old crumpled sari and with her hair undone. Her relatives sat outside in the courtyard with their belongings scattered around them, ready to move in upstairs. Bhuaji's old husband sat on his little bundle and had a nap in the sun.

'Only pray,' Bhuaji whispered into Durga's ear. 'With prayer He will surely come to you.' Durga's eyes were shut; perhaps she was asleep. 'As a son and as a lover,' Bhuaji whispered. The relatives talked gaily among themselves outside; they were in a good, almost a festive mood.

It seemed Durga was not asleep after all, for suddenly she got up and unlocked her steel almira. She took out everything – her silk saris, her jewellery, her cash-box. From time to time she smiled to herself. She was thinking of her husband and of his anger, his impotent anger, at thus seeing everything given away at last. The more she thought of him, the more vigorously she emptied her almira. Her arms worked with a will, flinging everything away in abandon, her hair fell into her face, perspiration trickled down her neck in runnels. Her treasure lay scattered in heaps and mounds all over the floor and Bhuaji squinted at it in avid surmise.

Durga said, 'Take it away. It is for you and for them —' and she jerked her head towards the courtyard where the relatives twittered like birds. Bhuaji was already squatting on the floor, sorting everything, stroking it with her hands in love and wonder. As she did so, she murmured approvingly to Durga: 'That is the way – to give up everything. Only if we give up everything will He come to us.' And she went on murmuring, while stroking the fine silks and running hard gold necklaces through her fingers: 'As a son and as a lover,' she murmured, over and over again, but absently.

The relatives were glad that Durga had at last come round and accepted her lot as a widow. They were glad for her sake. There was no other way for widows but to lead humble, bare lives; it was for their own good. For if they were allowed to feed themselves on the pleasures of the world, then they fed their own passions too, and that which should have died in them with the deaths of their husbands would fester and boil and overflow into sinful channels. Oh yes, said the relatives, wise and knowing, nodding their heads, our ancestors knew what they were doing when they laid down these rigid rules for widows; and though nowadays perhaps, in these modern times, one could be a little more lenient – for instance, no one insisted that Durga should shave her head – still, on the whole, the closer one followed the old traditions, the safer and the better it was.

THE ALIENS

PEGGY woke up to the sounds of a quarrel. There was
nothing unusual in this, for there was a quarrel every morning and it usually woke her up. Everyone in the house had
a very loud voice.

But by the time she was up and dressed, it was all over.
Her sister-in-law and mother-in-law sat peacefully together
at one end of the big dining-room table and drank tea out
of their saucers. Neither of them had had her bath yet, and
consequently both looked somewhat bedraggled, with their
thick long hair coming down and the crumpled saris in
which they had slept all night. Peggy, on the other hand,
already looked crisp and smart in her printed house-dress
and with her sensible short hair nicely brushed.

Peggy's husband, Dev, sat at the other end of the dining-
table, eating a breakfast of lentils, puris, pickles and fried
vegetables. His brother's children stood round his chair and
from time to time he put morsels of food into their mouths.
He pretended not to notice Peggy coming in but lowered his
head over his tray and ate more quickly, as if in a hurry to
finish everything before she could stop him. His mother,
sucking her tea, encouraged him: 'Eat, son, eat,' so that
Peggy couldn't say anything and had to content herself with
getting angry with him in her mind ('go on then, you greedy
piggy you, *get* fat').

Sarla, the sister-in-law, yawned without putting her hand
in front of her mouth – she had wonderful teeth and a very
pink tongue and palate – and before she had quite finished

yawning, she remarked, 'He always says himself the summer is a slack season.'

'Slack or no slack,' the mother-in-law said, 'the business must be attended to.'

Peggy said to the servant, in English, 'I think I'll have my scrambled egg now.'

'Bring her egg!' shouted the mother-in-law, who did not care for anyone else to give orders in the house. 'My boys are not like that – to run off on holidays when the business is there.'

Sarla yawned again, contemptuously this time.

'Business first, then pleasure, that is how they have been brought up,' the mother-in-law said and emphatically banged the lids of the huge silver cruet up and down.

'Wider!' said Dev to the children round his chair as he popped bits of puri into their already wide-open mouths. 'How he spoils them,' Peggy thought; everyone in the house spoiled the children, but he was the worst. When they had some of their own, she would certainly have to put her foot down. *Her* children (when they came) were not going to be brought up like Sarla's.

Sarla's husband, Suraj, came in, roaring to the servant for his breakfast. He was seconded by his mother who clapped her hands and shouted into the kitchen, 'Here is my boy hungry for his food and the do-nothings are sitting with their hands folded!'

Sarla at once turned on her husband: 'Because you pretend to be so busy, I must melt here in the heat all through the summer!'

'Oh-ho,' said the mother-in-law, 'now we are very delicate, a real memsahib.'

'Let her talk,' said Suraj, carelessly smiling, 'it is her morning mood.'

His wife sat upright and darted eyes of fire at him: 'It is not business that keeps you here, it is something quite different!' The smile went from his face.

'What are you suggesting against my son?' shouted the mother-in-law. Peggy's egg arrived, but she wished she could go somewhere else to eat it.

'He knows,' said Sarla. 'My God, who doesn't know, everybody knows! While I sit here all day looking after my children – Bubu! O Bubu! Have you drunk your milk? Munna! Tutsu! – I sit here yes day in day out, where do I ever go? what pleasure do I have in life! While *he* —'

'What evil fate has brought such a woman into our house?' cried the mother-in-law.

'It is *my* evil fate that has brought me here!' Mother and daughter-in-law, intent now only on one another, had jumped up and stood face to face. They were both large and splendidly developed women. The mother was not old yet, and ruling over her household had kept her, despite her widowhood, in health and strength. Her hair was still as black and abundant as Sarla's, and the sari, which had in her excitement slipped from her shoulder, revealed a fresh womanly cleft.

Suraj exhorted them: 'Fight fight, go on – it is the way for mothers and daughters-in-law.' He laughed and went on quite calmly eating his breakfast.

Peggy finished the last of her egg; she didn't feel like having her usual toast and marmalade, though she knew she would be hungry later if she didn't have it now. She went into her marital bedroom, which was the only place she and Dev had to themselves in the house. She sat on the bed, with her hands folded in her lap. She could hear Sarla and the mother-in-law shouting, and after a while Suraj joined in too. It was just like what had woken her up in the morning. She felt miserable and thought of home. No one at home ever fought like that; sometimes, of course, they had their little differences of opinion – especially on washing-days, Mum did tend to get a bit out of temper then – but they never forgot themselves. Only lower-class people forgot themselves and shouted the way they shouted in this house. She was thankful that Mum and Daddy couldn't hear them, they wouldn't know what to think. Sometimes she herself didn't know what to think.

Dev came in and he looked at her, a bit guilty, because of all the breakfast he had eaten. But she no longer cared about that.

She said, 'Why do they always have to quarrel and shout so loud?' They were still at it and could be heard quite clearly, but Dev said, surprised, 'Who?'

Peggy sighed and looked out of the window. The garden, the street beyond it, everything lay dead and still under the white-hot sun. She said, 'I can't see why we can't have a little place to ourselves. Just a couple of rooms, that's all we need.'

Dev was embarrassed – they had been over this before and had failed to see each other's point of view. He straightened his bush-shirt, looked at his watch: 'Time for office.'

'Where at least I could get a bit of peace and quiet to myself.' She took out a clean handkerchief and put it into his shirt-pocket and then she combed his hair with a little comb while he obediently lowered his head for her. 'It's never any use living with your in-laws,' she said, worldly-wise. There was no point in saying more – he never understood – but all the same she added, 'And when we get a baby, you see, I want to bring it up my own way.'

He became shy: 'Are you unwell?'

'Of course not, I just meant *suppose*.'

Suraj shouted to him from outside the door: 'For God's sake, let us get to office, she is eating my head up here!'

'When there is anything to be discussed, he runs to office!' Sarla cried.

'You'd better go then,' Peggy said wearily, and wearily she offered her cheek to him. Dev kissed it in the same way he always did—quickly, foolishly, and with an anxious look round as if to make sure no one was looking.

Peggy stayed in the bedroom and tidied up her undies. Not that they needed it, but only for something to do. That was the worst of having all those servants—there was never anything to do. Sometimes Peggy just longed to roll up her sleeves and get down to something, even if it was only polishing the floor. But of course, she couldn't, it would look bad and make everyone think she came from a low-class family. Once, a year ago, when she had first come and had only been here a month or two, she had tried to clean a window. She had seen it was dirty and instead of telling anyone about it, she had just taken a wet cloth and climbed up on the sill. Goodness, what a fuss when her mother-in-law had caught her at it! The things she had suggested about Peggy's family; and how Peggy had cried.

She felt like crying now, but she went on patiently folding and tidying. She smoothed her pink lace bra (her best) and recalled, as she did so, the occasion on which she had bought it. It had been during her lunch-hour—she was still working, she went on working right up till the last day: she just couldn't bear to leave the office where she had been working these eight years, ever since she left school (they had had such times together, she and Carole the other typist and Mrs. Temple the accountant and Jimmy the office-boy, and they all said, even the boss, they wouldn't know what they'd do without her). She always went out for her shopping

during her lunch-hour, and that particular day had been a
lovely warm spring one and she had been so happy, thinking
of Dev and how she was soon to be a bride. She couldn't
resist telling the girl who served her how she was buying
the bra to take with her out to India; and the girl said well
she never, and then she confided how she too was engaged,
to a boy she had gone to school with, and they both lived
out in Sheldon where he worked in a garage and now they
were looking for a couple of unfurnished rooms near there
so that they could be married. Peggy wished her luck and
she wished Peggy luck, and they both smiled at one another's good fortune; but afterwards, leaving the shop with
her purchase done up in a dainty parcel, Peggy couldn't
help thinking how much more romantic and exciting
her own future looked and what a lucky girl she really
was.

She put on the fan as fast as it would go and lay down on
the bed. She opened the top buttons of her house-dress and
hitched it up over her thighs and lay there relaxed and pant-
ing a bit with heat. Suddenly the two older children came
bursting in, chasing each other round and round the room,
laughing and making a lot of noise and not taking any
notice of Peggy at all. She pulled down her dress and
fumbled quickly to do up the buttons. 'I've told you again
and again,' she said without much hope, 'to knock before
coming in.'

'Time!' cried Munna. 'I've got hiccoughs!' 'No time!'
cried Bubu and they began to pull each other's hair. Sarla
could be heard shouting for them from another part of the
house. She came slapping in her slippers over the marble
floors: 'Bubu! Munna! Why haven't you gone for your bath!'
They ran past her and she began to yell for the Ayah,
demanding what was the Ayah doing not looking after the

children, what else was she kept there for and paid a fat salary and eating and drinking enough for ten? The Ayah came hurrying out of the kitchen (where she had been enjoying a leisured glass of tea), wiping her mouth with the end of her sari and pointing out how day and night she was running here and there on her feet and who was there could point a finger at her to say she ever slackened in her duties for one minute even? She was answered by both Sarla and by the mother-in-law, who was just having her bath, but, nothing daunted, shouted lustily from out of the bathroom amid the splash of water she was pouring over herself.

Sarla came into Peggy's room and began to pull out drawers and ruffle absent-mindedly through Peggy's things. She meant no harm and Peggy tried not to mind, though this was hard for her.

Sarla was grumbling. She grumbled about the Ayah and then about the heat and then she said, 'It is high time we were all gone to the hills.'

'It would be nice to go somewhere cool,' Peggy agreed, nervously watching while Sarla pulled out one of her neatly-folded nylon blouses.

'What else have I been saying day after day?' She held the blouse against herself, then impatiently tossed it aside and pulled out another, a pretty lime-green. 'But of course, whatever I say, he has to say something else, who ever listens to me? All these colours are so dull, you must write to your family and tell them to send new things for you.' She was going through the whole lot now and they lay scattered over the dressing-table and some trailed on to the floor. 'The children are suffering in the heat, but what is that to him? All he cares for now is that girl in the office in her frock with all her legs showing —' She made a sound of rage and contempt. 'She is as black as a boot, but still she must wear a frock and pretend to be English. Where is your nail-polish?' She tugged at a few more drawers, so that Peggy thought it wiser to get up and give it to her. 'He thinks it is wonderful to see fat girls in short skirts – it is all right for you to wear such things, Peggy, but for our Indian girls, even if they are only Anglo-Indian, it is very ugly and they only do it so that men will look with big eyes and think how nice.' She was sitting on the bed and daubing herself wildly with Peggy's nail-polish, so that some of it spilled on to the embroidered bedcover. 'They are all like that, everything is nice except only their own wives. Oh, how hot it is, how I am suffering with heat!' She wiped herself with the end of her sari, her face, her neck, her naked chest above the blouse. 'I must go away to the hills, it is for the sake of my health.' She had painted a few nails and held them up to study them. 'It is a very pale colour, Peggy, you must get a red-red, then one can see and enjoy. The day a girl is married is a day for rejoicing, but if we could see into the future we would know it is not joy but on the contrary sadness and sorrow that we should be feeling.'

Peggy felt like sighing with her, but instead she said in a bright brave little voice: 'We must all take our ups and downs as they come'; and remembered, as soon as she had said it, that it was her mother's phrase and she could almost hear her saying it (standing sturdily in lisle stockings and black shoes at the table in the living-room, with the iron in her hand and testing it against her cheek).

'I don't like your English proverbs, I think they sound very silly. Please don't imagine your husband is any better than mine, because in that way they are all the same.'

Peggy, tidying away her blouses, stood stock-still by the open drawer: 'I don't think it's fair to say that.'

'It is the truth, you will soon learn. You are not blind,
you can see for yourself how every time there is a pretty girl,
he also —'

'Dev is not like that at all.'

'They are all like that. Why are you crying?'

'I am not crying, Sarla.'

'There are tears in your eyes, I can see. Go on, cry, it is
nothing to be ashamed. There is enough to cry in everyone's
life, and here we are dying with heat because our husbands
are too busy with other women to take us away to the hills.'
The mother-in-law, emerging from her bathroom, could be
heard calling for them. 'And that old one, to have her on
our heads day and night!'

'We're here, Mama!' Peggy obediently called.

Later they all three sat in the drawing-room and the
servants brought them tea and fritters and sweetmeats.
Peggy was hungry, having missed her toast and marmalade,
but she cared neither for the fritters, which were stuffed
with chillis, nor for the sweetmeats which oozed ghee and
syrup. Sarla and the mother-in-law were in a good mood
with each other; they were discussing a forthcoming wedding which promised to be a very fine affair with two bands
and cooks specially brought from Lucknow. Sarla wondered
whether to wear her gold brocade sari or her silver and
crimson one; she was certainly decided on her diamond
necklace, but as for ear-rings, she was still wavering between
her turquoise drop ones, her pearl clusters or her ruby
pagodas. Her mother-in-law gave her good advice and they
discussed these pleasant possibilities for a while. Then the
mother-in-law said, 'And Peggy?' and they both looked at
her.

Peggy said, 'I think I'll go in my coffee lace and taffeta skirt.'

'No, you must certainly wear one of your saris,' the mother-in-law said. 'How will it look — people will say we have not given this girl who has come into our family any good saris.'

'The purple one from Mysore,' Sarla said.

'Or the gold tissue I had specially brought from Benares,' the mother-in-law said.

'They're both pretty,' Peggy said cautiously. She couldn't explain that she cared for neither of them; nor indeed for any of the other saris she had been given. Of course, she could see they were expensive and perhaps they would look well on someone else: on someone like Sarla, for instance. But for herself she liked something more quiet (she had always gone in for pale greens and powder blues and liked dresses with Peter-Pan collars and little bows on them). Besides, she couldn't quite manage the sari yet and tended to trip over it every now and again.

The others were looking at her critically: 'Of course, she is too pale for the gold.'

'Also too thin.' They both kept on looking at her, and then they both burst out laughing. 'What is the matter with you English girls?' the mother-in-law cried, 'you have nothing up here at all!'

'Or here!' laughed Sarla, slapping herself heartily on both massive hips so that they shook.

Peggy flushed palely, an English rose: 'We like to keep trim. It's the fashion these days.'

Sarla flung back her head and showed all her strong white teeth laughing: 'Our men would have something to say to us if we made such a fashion!' The mother-in-law gave her a push and they clutched each other and rocked backwards

and forwards and couldn't speak for some time. Peggy sat
by, bravely smiling with them.

'No,' said the mother-in-law, sobering at last, 'but she is a
good girl.' She wiped her eyes and sighed. 'My poor son.
You must eat more, child, eat and get strong. Every morning
one seer milk and two-three fried parathas with ghee, then
you will soon see the difference. And then the babies will
start to come also, otherwise what chance has a weak girl
like you of getting babies? Ayah! O Ayah! My legs are
hurting!'

Sarla plucked pins out of her hair so that slowly, like a
snake unwinding, that heavy black mass fell down over her
shoulders. 'My Bubu was born eleven months after. And
before he had given up my milk, Munna came, God bless
him. There was not much time wasted with us.' She watched
the Ayah who squatted on the floor and massaged the
mother-in-law's legs. 'When she has finished with you, she
can press my head. It is hurting.'

The children were playing at trains. They pushed all the
tall chairs with carved legs into rows and jumped up and
down over the upholstery. Peggy had to look the other
way; she couldn't bear to see good furniture treated that
way.

'It is the heat that is making my head hurt,' Sarla said. 'I
am not used to staying down in the plains at this time of
year.'

The mother-in-law stretched out her other leg for the
Ayah: 'And what happened to you when you were living in
your father's house, I would like to know.'

Sarla reared up immediately: 'Every year, as soon as
April came, Papa sent us away to the hills, this was the rule
in our house.'

The mother-in-law gave a snort of unbelief. 'Higher,' she

told the Ayah and hitched up her sari to her thigh, exposing a pale leg, hairy though well-shaped.

'We took a cook with us and rented a cottage!'

'All that costs money. Just here – aah, *there*.'

'In *my* family, money was never any consideration. We lived in very good style.'

'What skin,' said the Ayah. 'Firm, like a young girl's.'

'The food that was eaten in our house! Two seers of meat were brought from the bazaar every day, and fish also, and chicken.'

'And so fair,' said the Ayah. 'Just like a Kashmiri.'

'As far as I remember,' said the mother-in-law, 'you were a thin girl when you married. It is only in this house, with good meals, that you have become proper.'

Sarla gave a great burst of exaggerated laughter: 'The meals on festive occasions in this house are not up to what we ate for our everyday food.'

The mother-in-law echoed that laugh: 'It is like the story of the mouse and the elephant.' She pushed the Ayah away and pulled down her sari. 'The mouse said to the elephant: "In *my* house everything is so big and so beautiful —"'

'If you want to tell stories, please tell to my children, I am not interested in listening to such things.'

Peggy slipped quietly out of the room. She went back to her bedroom, but the children were now lying on the bed, on their stomachs and with arms outstretched, pretending to be aeroplanes. She sat down at the dressing-table and took out her writing-paper. There were a number of letters she ought to be writing – to her aunt Elsie and to her married friend Doreen; and to Mum and Daddy too, she hadn't written for over two weeks and they might be getting worried. But she didn't feel like writing letters. When she had first come, she had loved writing home and telling them all about the big white house she lived in, with the expensive furniture and a chandelier in the drawing-room, the servants and the garden which had a full-time gardener in it, the two cars and the chauffeur. . . . But now she no longer knew what to write. It wasn't as if anything ever happened, or as if she went out anywhere – except sometimes for drives in the evening, with the whole family, or shopping with the mother-in-law and Sarla, or to the houses of relatives when it was a festival day or there was a wedding on or someone had died.

The children were now crash-landing, so that Peggy had to take her writing-paper and go and sit in the study. No one ever did any studying there, but there was a big desk with a presentation inkstand on which was engraved in gold lettering : 'To our highly-esteemed boss, in honour of his fiftieth birthday. May God shower blessings for a hundred years more. From the employees of Naraian Motors.' It had been given to her late father-in-law. She had never met him, but over the desk there was a picture of him which she often studied. He looked rather like Dev, except that he had a much firmer mouth and chin and was a lot fatter. The way Dev was going, it probably wouldn't take him long to get as fat as his father; but he would never get a mouth and chin like that or such a (secretly she said it to herself) mean look in his eyes. It was the father who had built up the business – and with it, the family, buying this house for them and stuffing it with furniture and silver and crockery and carpets and pictures on the walls and every-thing else that he saw people with money usually bought for themselves. From all accounts, he had been a man with a lot of drive and go – Suraj was probably the one that took after him the most. She had to admit that poor Dev didn't have much drive or go: but, good heavens, that was what she had liked about him from the first, his being quiet and shy and not much caring what went on, so why should she complain now? All the same, she found herself ready to spill a few tears, so she was quite firm with herself and said '*Peggy*', the way Mum might have said it if she'd been there; and started writing 'Dear Mum and Daddy, Well here we are again . . .'

Suraj and Dev came home for lunch, which was a very big meal with mounds of rice and pickles and several kinds of curries. Peggy was getting more used to the hot food now, though it still made her eyes water and her nose run; and certainly, she would never be able to dig in with the same relish as the others – for one thing, she didn't have their kind of appetite, for another, she had been taught to eat daintily and with her mouth shut. The children also sat at the table, with the Ayah hovering above them, alternately coaxing them to eat and threatening them with what would happen to them if they didn't.

Sarla, leaning on the table with her elbow, her hair coming down over her face, never looked up except occasionally to throw dark glances at her husband; which he ignored with such insulting ease that soon she was throwing out more explicit hints: 'All morning my head has been hurting but who is there to ask are you well, are you ill, who is there to care what happens to me?'

The mother-in-law stroked Suraj's shoulder and said sweetly, 'Eat son, eat in peace,' though he hardly needed this encouragement. He leaned forward and helped himself to pickle. 'Poor boy, how hard he has been working all morning in the office.'

'Today we got our consignment of station wagons,' he said. 'They have been delayed four months.'

'Four months!' echoed the mother with exaggerated sympathy. 'So much trouble – trouble and worry, that is how it is in business.'

'And that girl with the fat legs, she is also trouble and worry?' Sarla said.

'Children who don't eat are taken away at night by the jackals,' warned the Ayah.

'Yes, I think it must be great trouble and worry to have someone like that in the office. It is so difficult to concentrate on the work. Oh my head, how it is aching.'

The mother-in-law pointed at Dev's plate and shouted at the servant: 'Where is the rice? Don't you see my son is waiting for more rice?'

Dev took a second helping and, as he did so, stole a guilty look at Peggy. She was sitting straight-backed on her chair, with her eyes lowered and lifting a fork to her lips; but he knew that she had noticed, so he said, placatingly, 'There is a nice English picture at the Regal. If you like, we can go one evening for the 6.30 show.'

'I will go with you,' Sarla said. 'There is no one else who will take me, so it is best for me to go with whoever I can.'

'Pictures are very bad for people whose head is hurting,' said the mother-in-law, waving away a fly that hovered over Suraj's plate.

Sarla came back at once: 'It is also very bad for people whose head is hurting to stay in the plains during the whole summer. In some cases this might even lead to very serious condition, such as tumour of the brain.'

'It would be best,' said Suraj innocently, 'if you were all to go away to the hills.'

Sarla glared at him: 'And you?'

'I will send the driver with you to take you up there and you can stay in a hotel.'

'They will come for you tonight, the jackals, just watch out!' cried the Ayah. Munna kicked the table so that his glass fell over and the water spread over the table and trickled on to the floor.

'I don't care for hotel food,' the mother-in-law said, 'it gives me a bad stomach.'

'That is what you are waiting for,' Sarla accused her husband. 'That we should go up there while you stay here and carry on as you like.'

He shrugged and called for a toothpick which the servant brought for him in a fluted silver container.

'I will never go!' Sarla cried. 'What quiet moment will I have up there, thinking thinking all the time of you down here with that —'

Some of the spilt water came trickling into Peggy's lap. She got up and murmured, 'Excuse me, please' – which was unnecessary but she made a point of keeping up her manners. She went back into the study where her writing-paper still lay on the desk. She sat down and suddenly she was writing very fast: 'Oh I can't tell you how fed up I am with it all and how awful it is and the heat and everyone shouting all the time and they are all so —' at which she stopped, not because there wasn't plenty more to say but because she wasn't sure whether the word she wanted was spelt c-o-r-s-e or c-o-a-r-s-e. And with this halt she came back to her senses, and tearing off the sheet of paper, crumpled it in her hand. She knew she would never send any such letter: how disappointed Mum and Daddy would be in her if they were ever to receive it. They would be worried too, of course, and sad for her, but most of all they would be disappointed. English people didn't behave like that, they never grumbled and moaned. Once they'd made their bed, they lay on it (that was another of Mum's phrases, and Peggy could just see her blue eyes grow bluer and her mouth grow tight as she said it – good old Mum, who never complained, even when the water-pipes froze and she had to climb up in the loft and unfreeze them with hot-water bottles and her fingers all swollen with the chilblains). It was only here that they grumbled all the time – about heat, headaches, husbands – if it wasn't one thing, then it was another, always some new grouse, always feeling sorry for themselves. That wasn't the way Peggy had been brought up; even when she was a baby, Mum never stood for any nonsense with her. And thinking of Mum, she felt ashamed of herself and tore the crumpled letter into many pieces which she dropped into her pocket.

Something was going on again. There were voices shouting and the children were crying and doors banged. She could hear Suraj's voice, loudest of all. He must have lost his temper with Sarla at last, and he was roaring like a bull. Sarla was shouting back at him and the mother-in-law shouted in between. Peggy tiptoed back into her bedroom and shut the door. Dev was lying on the bed, on the cover which he had failed to turn down, and was dropping off to sleep; noise never disturbed him. She neatly turned back the cover of her own bed and lay beside him. He pretended to be fast asleep.

How fat he was getting. He had been such a slim young boy when she had first seen him and knew him only as that nice Indian student who lodged with Doreen's mother. She looked at him and suddenly said, 'At least cut down on the rice.' He gave no sign, so she said, quite sharply, 'Don't pretend, dear.'

He opened his eyes. He had beautiful eyes – large and

dark and with a dreamy look in them; and how often she
and Doreen had commented on his lashes – fit for a girl,
they had always said, and sometimes, when she had wanted
to tease him, Doreen had told him: 'I'm going to a dance
tonight – can I wear your lashes?' Even now, when he had
grown so fat and his face already showed what he would
look like when he was middle-aged, his eyes remained as
they had been. She put out her hand and touched his cheek;
he went off to sleep again, so she removed her hand and
turned her back to him, and felt bitter.

Perhaps Sarla was right. She had herself noticed it long
ago, whenever they went out, that every time he saw a girl
he turned his head right round and looked at her. Of course,
they all did it, all the men to all the women, all of them
stared without any shame or embarrassment: it was just
one of the ways in which they were different from English
people. But he had been to England, he had had a nice
education and ought to know better – 'Hasn't anyone ever
told you,' she said, still with her back to him, 'that it's rude
to stare at people?'

He was so startled that he forgot to pretend to be asleep:
'But Peggy, I am not staring at you, my eyes are shut.'

'You do it even to Sarla. When she's come out of the
bathroom and her hair's down and you know she's got
nothing on under her sari – I've seen you with my own
eyes.'

'Peggy, you are imagining.'

'Just because she's fat, that's why you like her.' She was
sitting up now and blowing her nose into her little handkerchief. 'In England we don't like fat people, we try to keep
slim —'

'But Peggy, I also like slim people, you know I do.' He
was stroking her back and making soothing noises at her

and she let herself be coaxed to lie by his side; the moment she had done so, he shut his eyes again. She put her handkerchief back into her pocket and felt the torn pieces of her letter to Mum and Daddy. They made her feel ashamed all over again. Really, she didn't know what had come over her: now she was getting into a nagging wife as well, and if there was one thing she'd always been warned against . . . 'I'm sorry, dear,' she whispered into his ear. 'It must be the heat.'

'Sleep sleep, go to sleep,' he murmured.

It was all Sarla's fault. How dare she suggest such a thing against Dev? As if he would ever dream of going with anyone else. Even back at home he hadn't been interested in girls, though there he could have had plenty (everyone knew what some of these factory girls were). But Dev didn't go in for that kind of thing. Why, he had even been too shy to ask her for a date, so that it was always she who had had to take the initiative, or Doreen asking them to make up a foursome with herself and her boy-friend. And he had never taken any liberties either, not even after they were engaged. He was a good boy – a nice steady type, with clean habits, as Mum and Doreen's mother and aunt Elsie and everyone had said; almost like one of our own boys, even if he was an Indian.

'I don't think Sarla is always a very nice person,' she told him. 'I don't like people who say things about other people, and having rows all the time. . . .' But she noticed that the shouting had stopped. Sarla and Suraj must have gone into their bedroom; perhaps they too were lying down together on the bed. She knew it was wicked of her, but she often thought of them lying together on the bed. Sometimes, when they came out of their room, she could see in their faces what they had been doing in there; and Sarla often had marks on her. It made her feel quite sick to think of them. They were both so large and smelt of perspiration and oil and they ate a lot and didn't know how to control themselves. It was true, Dev also ate a lot but he knew how to control himself in that other thing; he knew she wasn't strong and he never made her do anything when she didn't want to do it.

'Are we going to the pictures tonight?' she said. 'If we are, I don't see why we should have to take Sarla with us. Why can't we be on our own for a change?'

He burped lightly in his sleep (that's what came of over-eating).

'Say pardon, dear,' she admonished him; but went on immediately – 'We're never on our own, only for sleeping. What's the use of being on our own only for sleeping?' She thought wistfully again of a little place all to themselves. She would make a lovely home. She would do all their own cooking and have a servant only for the cleaning. She would cook roast-meat and Yorkshire pudding and sausage and mash and treacle pudding. . . .

She felt the tears welling up and gave herself a mental little slap. Lying there, dreaming, in the middle of the day, wishing for the moon – 'what you need, my girl, is a good shaking.' She got up and washed her face and brushed her hair good and hard. 'Time to go back to the office!' she called to Dev. 'Upsy-daisy!'

'Already?' he grunted, out of his half-sleep.

'Come on, lazy-bones.'

Sarla and Suraj came out of their bedroom at the same time as they did. Sarla's blouse was half open and she had that special look on her face, a sort of fed, smiling look. She walked slowly and with a swagger of her hips, as if she knew she was being stared at and appreciated; and really, Suraj was staring at her as she walked in front of him and he was smiling to himself. Peggy turned round sharply and – yes, of course, as she had suspected, Dev was looking too with those nasty sort of eyes with which he looked at other women.

Sarla accompanied them down to the car. She was in a bantering mood and said, 'Please don't work too hard in the office and harm yourself.' Neither of the two men answered her but both were smiling. She watched them driving off, standing on the steps of the veranda with her hands on her hips; she called after them, 'Think of your wives and take good care of yourselves!' Then with a laugh she swaggered back into the house, giving a little skip on the last step. She went into her room and called to Peggy to come and talk to her. Peggy went reluctantly. She didn't like Sarla's room, it was always so untidy and smelled of Sarla. Clothes she had worn lay scattered about and on the dressing-table stood rows of Indian scent with ancient heavy smells of jasmine, rose and khas, and several lipsticks, some of which had their tops missing and were melting in the heat.

Sarla lay on her stomach across the bed and played with her youngest child, a fat black little boy with curly hair. She prodded him and tickled him so that he rolled to and fro on the bed and doubled up with laughter. Peggy warned, 'Better be careful, he might bring up his dinner.'

'Oh my star, you fat little moon-flower,' said Sarla, tickling him under the arms. To Peggy she said, 'We must get a room-cooler, then it will be more comfortable for the children.'

'Aren't we going to the hills?'

Sarla only laughed and bit her son's plump arm so that he shrieked.

The mother-in-law, just up from her sleep, with bleary eyes and crumpled sari, stood in the doorway, scratching her elbow: 'My sons have gone back to office?'

'They work *so* hard,' Sarla laughed. Her mother-in-law glanced at her suspiciously and saw the look on her face and the half-open blouse with her breasts swelling out of it. 'Do up your blouse,' she said crossly, 'have you no shame, with the servants walking about?' She sank down on the edge of the bed, slow and heavy like an old woman. Peggy had often noticed that, after Sarla had been with Suraj and looked the way she looked now, the mother-in-law turned herself into an old woman. She sat and sighed – 'Such heat, it is too much for me to bear.'

'We were just talking how we must get a room-cooler,' Sarla said cheerfully.

'What use is such a thing to us? We must get away to the hills, for our own health and that of the children. Ai-ai, I am aching all over.'

'Shall I call Ayah for massage?'

'The boys can stay here and once or twice they will come for week-end.'

Sarla said, 'He doesn't want me to go.'

'Doesn't want you to go! Perhaps you think my son can't live his life without you?'

Sarla buried her face in her child's stomach and gave a laugh of delight from out of there.

'It is necessary for me to go,' the mother-in-law said. 'If my husband were still with us, God rest his soul, he would have made all arrangements long ago. He was always very careful of my health and comforts.' She wiped the corners of her eyes with the end of her sari. 'It is better to be dead than to stay in life after your husband has departed. Do up your blouse!'

Sarla glanced down at herself and smiled at what she saw.

'I don't know how you behaved in your father's house but while you are living in my house you will dress like a woman of decent family. And you also,' she turned on Peggy. 'These frocks of yours may be all right where you have come from, but here we don't like to see someone show half her body. Tomorrow, when we start our packing, see that you leave all these frocks behind and take only the saris I have given.'

'Who is packing tomorrow?' Sarla said.

'We are all packing. By Thursday we shall go away. I have had enough of heat now.'

'My husband won't allow me to go.'

'Who is your husband to allow or not allow, when your mother-in-law is here? Perhaps I am already dead that all of you think you can do as you please!'

'I shall always do as my husband pleases, no one else,' said Sarla.

Peggy went quietly back to her own room. She shut her door, but she could still hear them. The fan churned up stale hot air, her head ached and perspiration trickled down her legs. She took out her writing-paper again and began to write with a firm hand: 'Dear Mum and Daddy, Well here we are again. It is a bit hot but we are keeping our chins up! There is talk about going away to the hills where it is nice and cool they say. . . .' She wrote with her back very straight and her lips very tight and pressing the nib so hard that it made little holes in the paper.

She didn't know this, but she looked at that moment very much like her Mum had looked twenty years ago (during the war, with Daddy away in the army) queuing up for the rations or carrying in the coal on a rainy English winter morning.

THE INTERVIEW

I AM always very careful of my appearance, so you could not say that I spent much more time than usual over myself that morning. It is true, I trimmed and oiled my moustache, but then I often do that; I always like it to look very neat, like Raj Kapoor's, the film star's. But I knew my sister-in-law and my wife were watching me. My sister-in-law was smiling, and she had one hand on her hip; my wife only looked anxious. I knew she was anxious. All night she had been whispering to me. She had whispered, 'Get this job and take me away to live somewhere alone, only you and I and our children.' I had answered, 'Yes,' because I wanted to go to sleep. I don't know where and why she has taken this notion that we should go and live alone.

When I had finished combing my hair, I sat on the floor and my sister-in-law brought me my food on a tray. It may sound strange that my sister-in-law should serve me, and not my wife, but it is so in our house. It used to be my mother who brought me my food, even after I was married; she would never allow my wife to do this for me, though my wife wanted to very much. Then, when my mother got so old, my sister-in-law began to serve me. I know that my wife feels deeply hurt by this, but she doesn't dare to say anything. My mother doesn't notice many things any more, otherwise she certainly would not allow my sister-in-law to bring me my food; she has always been very jealous of this privilege herself, though she never cared who served my brother. Now she has become so old that she can hardly see anything, and most of the time she sits in the corner by the family trunks and folds and strokes her pieces of cloth. For years now she has been collecting pieces of cloth. Some of them are very old and dirty, but she doesn't care, she loves them all equally. Nobody is allowed to touch them. Once there was a great quarrel, because my wife had taken one of them to make a dress for our child. My mother shouted at her – it was terrible to hear her: but then, she has never liked my wife – and my wife was very much afraid and cried and tried to excuse herself. I hit her across the face, not very hard and not because I wanted to, but only to satisfy my mother. The old woman kept quiet then and went back to folding and stroking her pieces of cloth.

All the time I was eating, I could feel my sister-in-law looking at me and smiling. It made me uncomfortable. I thought she might be smiling because she knew I wouldn't get the job for which I had to go and be interviewed. I also knew I wouldn't get it, but I didn't like her to smile like that. It was as if she were saying, 'You see, you will always have to be dependent on us.' It is clearly my brother's duty to keep me and my family until I can get work and contribute my own earnings to the family household. There is no need for her to smile about it. But it is true that I am more dependent on her now than on anyone else. Since my mother has got so old, my sister-in-law has become more and more the most important person in the house, so that she even keeps the keys and the household stores. At first I didn't like this. As long as my mother managed the household, I was sure of getting many extra tit-bits. But now I find that my sister-in-law is also very kind to me – much more kind than she is to her husband. It is not for him that she saves the tit-bits, nor for her children, but for me; and when she gives them to me, she never says anything and I never say anything, but she smiles and then I feel confused and rather embarrassed. My wife has noticed what she does for me.

I have found that women are usually kind to me. I think they realize that I am a rather sensitive person and that therefore I must be treated very gently. My mother has always treated me very gently. I am her youngest child, and I am fifteen years younger than my brother who is next to me (she did have several children in between us, but they all died). Right from the time when I was a tiny baby, she understood that I needed greater care and tenderness than other children. She always made me sleep close beside her in the night, and in the day I usually sat with her and my grandmother and my widowed aunt, who were also very fond of me. When I got bigger, my father sometimes wanted to take me to help in his stall (he had a little grocer's stall, where he sold lentils and rice and cheap cigarettes and coloured drinks in bottles) but my mother and grandmother and aunt never liked to let me go. Once he did take me with him, and he made me pour some lentils out of paper bags into a tin. I rather liked pouring the lentils – they made such a nice noise as they landed in the tin – but suddenly my mother came and was very angry with my father for making me do this work. She took me home at once, and when she told my grandmother and aunt what had happened, they stroked me and kissed me and then they gave me a hot fritter to eat. The fact is, right from childhood I have been a person who needs a lot of peace and rest, and my food too has to be rather more delicate than that of other people. I have often tried to explain this to my wife, but as she is not very intelligent, she doesn't seem to understand.

Now my wife was watching me while I ate. She was squatting on the floor, washing our youngest baby; the baby's head was in her lap, and all one could see of it was the back of its legs and its naked bottom. My wife did not watch me as openly as my sister-in-law did; only from time to time she raised her eyes to me, I could feel it, and they were very worried and troubled. She too was thinking about the job for which I was going to be interviewed, but she was anxious that I should get it. 'We will go and live somewhere alone,' she had said. Why did she say it? When she knows that it is not possible and never will be.

And even if it were possible, I would not like it. I can't live away from my mother; and I don't think I would like to live away from my sister-in-law. I often look at her and it makes me happy. Even though she is not young any more, she is still beautiful. She is tall, with big hips and big breasts and eyes that flash; she often gets angry, and when she is angry, she is the most beautiful of all. Then her eyes are like fire and she shows all her teeth which are very strong and white, and her head is proud with the black hair flying loose. My wife is not beautiful at all. I was very disappointed in her when they first married me to her. Now I have got used to her and I even like her, because she is so good and quiet and never troubles me at all. I don't think anybody else in our house likes her. My sister-in-law always calls her 'that beauty', but she does not mean it; and she makes her do all the most difficult household tasks, and often she shouts at her and even beats her. This is not right; my wife has never done anything to her – on the contrary, she always treats her with respect. But I cannot interfere in their quarrels.

Then I was ready to go, though I didn't want to go. I knew only too well what would happen at the interview. My mother blessed me, and my sister-in-law looked at me over her shoulder and her great eyes flashed with laughter. I didn't look at my wife, who still sat squatting on the floor, but I knew she was pleading with me to get the job like she had pleaded in the night. As I walked down the stairs, the daughter of the carpenter, who lives in one of the rooms on the lower floor, came out of her door and she walked up the stairs as I walked down, and she passed very close beside me, with her eyes lowered but her arm just touching my sleeve. She always waits for me to come out and then she passes me on the stairs. We have never spoken together. She is a very young girl, her breasts are only just forming; her blouse has short sleeves and her arms are beautiful, long and slender. I think soon she is to be married, I have heard my sister-in-law say so. My sister-in-law laughed when she told me, she said, 'It is high time' and then she said something coarse. Perhaps she has noticed that the girl waits for me to pass on the stairs.

No, I did not want to go to the interview. I had been to so many during the last few months, and always the same things happened. I know I have to work, in order to earn money and give it to my mother or my sister-in-law for the household, but there is no pleasure for me in the work. Last time I had work it was in an insurance office and all day they made me sit at a desk and write figures. What pleasure could there be for me in that? I am a very thoughtful person, and I like always to sit and think my own thoughts; but while I thought my own thoughts in the office, I sometimes made mistakes over the figures and then my superiors were very angry with me. I was always afraid of their anger, and I begged their forgiveness and admitted that I was much at fault. When they forgave me, I was no longer afraid and I continued doing my work and thinking my thoughts. But the last time they would not forgive me again, though I begged and begged and cried what a faulty, bad man I was and what good men they were, and how they were my mother and my father and how I looked only to them for my life and the lives of my children. But when they still said I must go, I saw that the work there was really finished and I stopped crying. I went into the washroom and combed my hair and folded my soap in my towel, and then I took my money from the accountant without a word and I left the office with my eyes lowered. But I was no longer afraid, because what is finished is finished, and my brother still had work and probably one day I would get another job.

Ever since then my brother has been trying to get me into government service. He himself is a clerk in government service and enjoys many advantages: every five years he gets an increase of ten rupees in his salary and he has ten days sick-leave in the year and when he retires he will get a pension. It would be good for me also to have such a job; but it is difficult to get, because first there is an interview at which important people sit at a desk and ask many questions. I am afraid of them, and I cannot understand properly what they are saying, so I answer what I think they want me to answer. But it seems that my answers are not after all the right ones, because up till now they have not given me a job.

On my way to this interview, I thought how much nicer it would be to go to the cinema instead. If I had had ten annas, perhaps I would have gone; it was just time for the morning show. The young clerks and the students would be collecting in a queue outside the cinema now. They would be standing and not talking much, holding their ten annas and waiting for the box-office to open. I enjoy these morning shows, perhaps because the people who come to them are all young men like myself, all silent and rather sad. I am often sad; it would even be right to say that I am sad most of the time. But when the film begins, I am happy. I love to see the beautiful women, dressed in golden clothes with heavy ear-rings and necklaces and bracelets covering their arms, and their handsome lovers who are all the things I would like to be. And when they sing their love-songs, so full of deep feelings, the tears sometimes come into my eyes; but not because I am sad, no, on the contrary, because I am so happy. After the film is over, I never go home straight away, but I walk around the streets and think about how wonderful life could be.

When I arrived at the place where the interview was, I had to walk down many corridors and ask directions from many peons before I could find the right room. The peons were all rude to me, because they knew what I had come for. They lounged on benches outside the offices, and when I asked them, they looked me up and down before answering, and sometimes they made jokes about me with one another. I was very polite to them, for even though they were only peons, they had uniforms and jobs and belonged here, and they knew the right way whereas I did not. At last I came to the room where I had to wait. Many others were already sitting there, on chairs which were drawn up all round the room against the wall. No one was talking. I also sat on a chair, and after a while an official came in with a list and he asked if anyone else had come. I got up and he asked my name, and then he looked down the list and made a tick with a pencil. He said to me very sternly, 'Why are you late?' I begged pardon and told him the bus in which I had come had had an accident. He said, 'When you are called for interview, you have to be here exactly on time, otherwise your name is crossed off the list.' I begged pardon again and asked him very humbly please not to cross me off this time. I knew that all the others were listening, though none of them looked at us. He was very stern with me and even scornful, but in the end he said, 'Wait here, and when your name is called, you must go in at once.'

I did not count the number of people waiting in the room, but there were many. Perhaps there was one job free, perhaps two or three. I knew that all the others were very worried and anxious to get the job, so I became worried and anxious too. The walls of the room were painted green half-way up and white above that and were quite bare. There was a fan turning from the ceiling, but it was not turning fast enough to give much breeze. Behind the big door the interview was going on; one by one we would all be called in behind this closed door.

I began to worry desperately. It always happens like this. When I come to an interview, I don't want the job at all, but when I see all the others waiting and worrying, I want it terribly. Yet at the same time I know that I don't want it. It would only be the same thing over again: writing figures and making mistakes and then being afraid when they found out. And there would be a superior officer to whom I would have to be very deferential, and every time I saw him or heard his voice I would begin to be afraid that he had found out something against me. For weeks and months I would sit and write figures, getting wearier of it and wearier, so that more and more I would be thinking my own thoughts. Then the mistakes would come, and my superior officer would be angry and I afraid.

My brother never makes mistakes. For years he has been sitting in the same office, writing figures and being deferential to his superior officer; he concentrates very hard on his work, and so he doesn't make mistakes. But all the same he is afraid; that is why he concentrates so hard – because he is afraid that he will make a mistake and they will be angry with him and take away his job. He is afraid of this all the time. And he is right: what would become of us all if he also lost his job? It is not the same with me. I think I am afraid to lose my job only because that is a thing of which one is expected to be afraid. When I have actually lost it, I am really relieved. But I am very different from my brother; even in appearance I am very different. It is true, he is fifteen years older than I am, but even when he was my age, he never looked like I do. My appearance has always attracted others, and up to the time I was married, my mother used to stroke my hair and my face and say many tender things to me. Once, when I was walking on my way to school through the bazaar, a man called to me, very softly, and when I came he gave me a ripe mango, and then he took me into a dark passage which led to a disused mosque, and he touched me under my clothes and he said, 'You are so nice, so nice.' He was very kind to me. I love wearing fine clothes, very thin white muslin kurtas which have been freshly washed and starched and are embroidered at the shoulders. Sometimes I also use scent, a fine khas smell; my hair-oil also smells of khas. Some years ago, when the carpenter's daughter was still a small child and did not yet wait for me on the stairs, there was a girl living in the tailor's shop opposite our house and she used to follow me when I went out. But it is my brother who is married to a beautiful wife, and my wife is not beautiful at all. He is not happy with his wife; when she talks to him, she talks in a hard scornful way; and it is not for him that she saves the best food, but for me, even though I have not brought money home for many months.

The big closed door opened and the man who had been

in there for interview came out. We all looked at him, but he walked out in a great hurry, with a preoccupied expression on his face; probably he was going over in his mind all that had been said at the interview. I could feel the anxiety in the other men getting stronger, so mine got stronger too. The official with the list came and we all looked at him. He read out another name and the man whose name was called jumped up from his chair; he did not notice that his dhoti had got caught on a nail in the chair and he wondered why he could not go farther. When he realized what had happened, he tried to disentangle himself, but his fingers shook so much that he could not get the dhoti off the nail. The official watched him and said, 'Hurry, now, do you think the gentlemen will wait for you for as long as you please?' Then the man also dropped the umbrella he was carrying and now he was trying both to disentangle the dhoti and to pick up the umbrella. When he could not get the dhoti loose, he became so desperate that he tore at the cloth and ripped it free. It was a pity to see the dhoti torn because it was a new one, which he was probably wearing for the first time and had put on specially for the interview. He clasped his umbrella to his chest and walked in a great hurry to the interviewing room, with his dhoti hanging about his legs and his face swollen with embarrassment and confusion.

We all sat and waited. The fan, which seemed to be a very old one, made a creaking noise. One man kept cracking his finger-joints – *tik*, we heard, *tik* (it made my own finger-joints long to be cracked too). All the rest of us kept very still. From time to time the official with the list came in, he walked round the room very slowly, tapping his list, and then we all looked down at our feet and the man who had been cracking his finger-joints stopped doing it. A faint and muffled sound of voices came from behind the closed door.

Sometimes a voice was raised, but even then I could not make out what was being said, though I strained very hard.

The last time I had an interview, it was very unpleasant for me. One of the people who was interviewing took a dislike to me and shouted at me very loudly. He was a large fat man and he wore an English suit; his teeth were quite yellow, and when he became angry and shouted, he showed them all, and even though I was very upset, I couldn't help looking at them and wondering how they had become so yellow. I don't know why he was angry. He shouted: 'Good God, man, can't you understand what's said to you?' It was true, I could not understand, but I had been trying so hard to answer well. What more did he expect of me? Probably there was something in my appearance which he did not like. It happens that way sometimes – they take a dislike to you, and then of course there is nothing you can do.

When I thought of the man with the yellow teeth, I became more anxious than ever. I need great calm in my life. Whenever anything worries me too much, I have to cast the thought of it off immediately, otherwise there is a danger that I may become very ill. All my limbs were itching so that it was difficult for me to sit still, and I could feel blood rushing into my brain. It was this room that was doing me so much harm: all the other men waiting, anxious and silent, and the noise from the fan and the official with the list walking round, tapping his list or striking it against his thigh, and the big closed door behind which the interview was going on. I felt great need to get up and go away. I didn't *want* the job. I wasn't even thinking about it any more – I was thinking only about how to avoid having to sit here and wait.

Now the door opened again and the man with the torn

new dhoti came out. He was biting his lip and scratching the back of his neck, and he too walked straight out without looking at us at all. The big door was left slightly open for a moment, and I could see a man's arm in a white shirtsleeve and part of the back of his head. His shirt was very white and of good material, and his ears stood away from his head so that one could see how his spectacles fitted into the backs of his ears. I realized at once that this man would be my enemy and that he would make things very difficult for me and perhaps even shout at me. Then I knew it was no use for me to stay there. The official with the list came back and great panic seized me that he would read out my name. I got up quickly, murmuring, 'Please excuse me – bathroom,' and went out. The official with the list called after me, 'Hey mister, where are you going?' so I lowered my head and walked faster. I would have started to run, but that might have caused suspicion, so I just walked as fast as I could, down the long corridors and right out of the building. There at last I was able to stop and take a deep breath, and I felt much better.

I stood still for only a little while, then I moved on though not in any particular direction. There were many clerks and peons moving around in the street, hurrying from one office building to another and carrying files and papers. Everyone seemed to have something to do. I was glad when I had moved out of this block and on to the open space where people like myself, who had nothing to do, sat under the trees or in any other patch of shade they could find. But I couldn't sit there; it was too close to the office blocks, and any moment someone might come and say to me, 'Why did you go away?' So I walked farther. I was feeling quite light-hearted; it was such a relief for me not to have to be interviewed.

I came to a row of eating-stalls, and I sat down on a wooden bench outside one of them, which was called the Paris Hotel, and asked for tea. I felt badly in need of tea, and since I intended to walk part of the way home, I was in a position to pay for it. There were two Sikhs sitting at the end of my bench, who were eating with great appetite, dipping their hands very rapidly into brass bowls. In between eating they exchanged remarks with the proprietor of the Paris Hotel, who sat high up inside his stall, stirring in a big brass pot in which he was cooking the day's food. He was chewing a betel leaf, and from time to time he spat out the red betel juice far over the cooking-pot and on to the ground between the wooden benches and tables.

I sat quietly at my end of the bench and drank my tea. The food smelt very good, and it made me realize that I was hungry. I decided that if I walked all the way home, I could afford a little cake (I am very fond of sweet things). The cake was not new, but it had a beautiful piece of bright-green peel inside it. On reaching home I would lie down at once to sleep and not wake up again till tomorrow morning. That way no one would be able to ask me any questions. I would not look at my wife at all, so I would be able to avoid her eyes. I would not look at my sister-in-law either; but she would be smiling, that I knew already – leaning against the wall with her hand on her hip, looking at me and smiling. She would know that I had run away, but she would not say anything.

Let her know! What does it matter? It is true I have no job and no immediate prospect of getting one. It is true that I am dependent on my brother. Everybody knows that. There is no shame in it: there are many people without jobs.

And she has been so kind to me up till now, there is no reason why she should not continue to be kind to me. Though I know she is not by nature a kind woman; she speaks mostly with a very harsh tongue and her actions also are harsh. Only to me she has been kind.

The Sikhs at the end of the bench had finished eating. They licked their fingers and belched deeply, the way one does after a good meal. They started to laugh and joke with the proprietor. I sat quiet and alone at my end of the bench. Of course they did not laugh and joke with me. They knew that I was superior to them, for whereas they worked with their hands, I am a lettered man who does not have to sweat for a living but sits on a chair in an office and writes figures and can speak in English. My brother is very proud of his superiority, and he has great contempt for carpenters and mechanics and such people who work with their hands. I am also proud of being a lettered man, but when I listened to the Sikhs laughing and joking, the thought came to me that perhaps their life was happier than mine. It was a thought that had come to me before. There is the carpenter who lives downstairs in our house, the one whose daughter waits for me on the stairs, and though he is poor, there is always great eating in his house and many people come and I hear them laughing and singing and even dancing. The carpenter is a big strong man and he always looks happy, never anxious and sick with worry the way my brother does. He doesn't wear shoes and clean white clothes like my brother and I do, nor does he speak any English, but all the same he is happy. Even though his work is inferior, I don't think he gets as weary of it as I do of mine, and he has no superior officer to make him afraid.

Then I thought again about my sister-in-law and I thought that if I were kind to her, she would continue to be kind to me. I became quite excited when I thought of being kind to her. I would know then how her big breasts felt under the blouse, how warm they were and how soft. And I would know about the inside of her mouth with the big strong teeth. Her tongue and palate are very pink, like the pink satin blouse she wears on festive occasions, and I had often wondered whether they felt as soft as the blouse too. Her eyes would be shut and perhaps there would be tears on the lashes; and she would be making warm animal sounds and her big body too would be warm like an animal's. I became very excited when I thought of it; but when the excitement had passed, I was sad. Because then I thought of my wife, who is thin and not beautiful and there is no excitement in her body. But she does whatever I want and always tries to please me. I remembered her whispering to me in the night, 'Take me away, let us go and live somewhere alone, only you and I and our children.' That can never be, and so always she will have to be unhappy.

I was very sad when I thought of her being unhappy; because it is not only she who is unhappy but I also and many others. Everywhere there is unhappiness. I thought of the man whose new dhoti had been torn and who would now have to go home and sew it carefully so that the tear would not be seen. I thought of all the other men sitting and waiting to be interviewed, all but one or two of whom would not get the job for which they had come to be interviewed, and so again they would have to go to another interview and another and another, to sit and wait and be anxious. And my brother who has a job, but is frightened that he will lose it; and my mother so old that she can only sit on the floor and stroke her pieces of cloth; and my sister-in-law who does not care for her husband; and the carpenter's daughter who is to be married and perhaps she also will not be happy. Yet life could be so different. When I go to the cinema and hear the beautiful songs they sing, I know how different it could be; and also sometimes when I sit alone and think my thoughts, then I have a feeling that everything could be so beautiful. But now my tea was finished and also my cake, and I wished I had not bought them, because it was a long way to walk home and I was tired.

A BIRTHDAY IN LONDON

MR. LUMBIK was the first guest to arrive, rather too early. He had a big bunch of flowers in tissue paper and wore a tweed jacket with leather buttons, which gave him a jaunty air. 'A happy birthday and so many of them,' he said, bending over her hand to kiss it with that special tender air he had adopted towards her.

Sonia was flustered – by his early arrival, by the flowers, by the tender air which she never knew how to deal with. She blushed, and this made her seem like a lovely young girl receiving her first suitor. 'Mr. Lumbik,' she said, 'you shouldn't. An old woman like me has no birthdays.'

'Ow, ow!' he cried, clutching his ears, which stood away from his head so that the light shone through them. 'They are hurting, hearing you speak such things!'

She laughed, all young and gay – 'You and your jokes, you should be ashamed, Mr. Lumbik.'

'One little birthday favour,' he begged, holding up one modest little finger. 'Just one little, little favour from the birthday child.'

She again became somewhat agitated. She hoped he wasn't going to ask for a kiss, though that was what she rather expected. She didn't want to kiss Mr. Lumbik at all – not even, bending down, to peck at his cheek, which was never shaved well enough for her liking.

'Not Mr. Lumbik,' he begged. 'Not ever again Mr. Lumbik. Karl.' He put his head to one side and looked up at her pleadingly out of pale little ageing eyes. 'All right? Karl. Such a nice name.'

She didn't reply. Instead she carried the *apfel strudel* from the kitchen into her room, where the table was laid for the birthday party. Mr. Lumbik followed her on soft crêpe soles. He didn't press for an answer. He prided himself on his knowledge of women: and Sonia was the type one had to proceed with gently and tactfully, for she was of very good family and had had a romantic upbringing.

'Now I have a surprise for you,' he said. 'You will be pleased to learn from me that now they have granted me my British citizenship.'

'How nice,' said Sonia, concentrating on the last-minute touches to her table. She had been a British citizen for ten years, and the thrill had worn off.

'Yes, a special telephone call from Scotland Yard.' He dialled an imaginary telephone and held an imaginary receiver to his ear. 'Hallo, Karl Lumbik? You are now a very small member of the very big British Commonwealth. God save the Queen, Karl Lumbik! God save the Queen, Mr. Scotland Yard!' The imaginary receiver was replaced and Mr. Lumbik stood at attention.

Sonia laughed: 'How funny you are.' Everything was a joke to him. If only Otto had been a bit more like that. But Otto had always taken everything very tragically. When they became British citizens, he had taken that tragically too. 'Yes, our passports they have given us,' he had said, 'but what else have we got?' 'Ottolein!' she had cried, 'be happy!' But no need to tell Karl Lumbik to be happy.

He was using his tender voice again. 'So now I am a very eligible cavalier, I think.' But it was the wrong note, he saw at once: she had turned away from him and was adjusting Otto's framed photograph on the table by her sleeping-

couch. 'I think again I have opened my big mouth too
wide,' he said ruefully, so that the defensive expression went
from her face and she couldn't help laughing. She never
could help laughing with him, he said such comic things.
She tried to be remote and dignified, but after all she was
the same Sonia Wolff, née Rothenstein, she had always
been. The big laughing girl, they had called her. She always
had been big – large bosom, large hips, though graceful
with it, a fine full-blown flower on slender stalk legs – and
she had been for ever laughing, or on the brink of laughter,
her short curved upper lip trembling over her healthy
teeth.

There was a ring at the door-bell, and Mr. Lumbik glided
out like an expert butler to open. 'Come in, come in,' he
said, bowing deeply at the entrance door, 'the *apfel strudel*
has come out very well.'

'Where is the birthday child?' cried Mrs. Gottlob in her
hoarse, uninhibited voice. It was a voice Sonia knew only
too well, for she had heard it often enough, screaming up
the stairs about lights that had been left burning and baths
that had not been cleaned after use; and Otto, on hearing it,
used to grow pale and very quiet, so that Sonia had to go
downstairs and be as charming as she could be, accepting
and admitting everything to stop Mrs. Gottlob from shouting and upsetting Otto. But, of course, all that was over now,
and Mrs. Gottlob was no longer the landlady but a friend.

She came in and gave Sonia a big smack of a kiss and a box
of chocolates. 'The kiss is for love and the chocolates for
eating,' she said.

The box was very large and ornate, tied with a blue satin
ribbon. It was just like the ones Otto had so often brought
for her in Berlin. He used to come tiptoeing into what they
called the morning-room, where she would be sitting at her

escritoire writing letters or answering invitations; and smiling and pleased, the box held roguishly behind his back, he would say, 'Let us see now what nice surprise there is for us today.' And she would jump up, all large and graceful and girlish: 'Oh Otto!'

'So,' said Mrs. Gottlob, sitting down with a creak and a groan, 'how does it feel like to be twenty-five?'

'Already twenty-five!' cried Mr. Lumbik, clasping his hands together in wonder.

'Even my baby, my Werner, is nearly twenty-six,' said Sonia, shining and proud as always when she spoke of either of her children.

'And where is he today, on Mutti's birthday?' demanded Mrs. Gottlob. 'Again out with the girl-friends, I think?' She shook an extremely fat forefinger: 'I know your Werner – a very bad boy.'

'If you are not a bad boy at twenty-six, then when can you be a bad boy?' said Mr. Lumbik. He gave a reminiscent smile: 'Ask them in Vienna about one Karl Lumbik at twenty-six – la, la, la,' and he swayed his head, thinking of the girls and the cafés and Karl Lumbik in a tilted hat and camel coat.

'Ask them in London about one Karl Lumbik at fifty-six,' Mrs. Gottlob retorted, 'the story will not be different, only it is an old good-for-nothing where once there was a young good-for-nothing.'

'You are giving me a bad reputation,' said Mr. Lumbik, not ill-pleased, running his hands down the lapels of his coat and rocking to and fro on his heels.

'I had a letter from my Lilo today,' Sonia said. 'My birthday letter – just think, all the way from Israel and it arrives exactly on the right day. And there are nice photos too.' She took down the letter from where it was propped proudly on the mantelpiece and showed Mrs. Gottlob the photos of Lilo and her husband – sun-burnt stocky farm-workers with open collars and rolled-up sleeves – and their blond naked baby.

'Ach, the lovely baby,' crooned Mrs. Gottlob lovingly into the photo. 'He is like your Werner, I think – I remember just like this your Werner's hair went when he was four years old and first came to live in my house.'

Mr. Lumbik peered over one of Mrs. Gottlob's shoulders and Sonia over the other. 'There is also something from my dear late Papa in him,' Sonia said, sighing for her father, a large, healthy, handsome man who had loved good living and had died at Auschwitz. 'And also, I think – you don't think so?' she asked timid and hopeful, 'of my dear late Otto – the eyes, you see, and the forehead, Otto had always such a wonderful forehead.'

Mr. Lumbik glanced towards Otto's photo by the sleeping-couch. The wonderful forehead, he thought, was mainly created by the absence of any hair on the head. He remembered Otto Wolff as a small, bald, shrinking man, very tired, very sick, very old, in an expensive German dressing-gown which had grown too big for him. Mr. Lumbik had always thought what a pity it was that a fine woman like Sonia couldn't have married something better. Though, of course, Otto Wolff had been a very wealthy factory-owner in Berlin, and it wasn't quite fair to judge him as he had been in his last years – only a poor refugee who couldn't speak English, had no work and lodged in Mrs. Gottlob's house.

'Yes, perhaps also our good Mr. Wolff,' said Mrs. Gottlob, considering the grandchild. 'What a fine gentleman he was – Lumbik, I always say, never have I had a fine gentleman like Mr. Wolff in my house.'

A little tear came into Sonia's eye, but she was smiling with pleasure. How good Mrs. Gottlob was! Sonia had always told Otto that she was a good woman, in spite of her loud voice and crude manners. But Otto was so sensitive; and, of course, he had always been used to refined people and it was difficult for him to adjust. The little tear ran down her cheek, and she wiped it away with her handkerchief monogrammed with S. 'Yes, Mrs. Gottlob,' she said, 'we will none of us see a fine gentleman like my dear late Otto again. Oh, if you had known him in Germany, when he had the factory and the villa in Charlottenburg, what a respect you would have had for him then!' Always so dapper and neat, in his well-cut suit made of the best English cloth, spats over his hand-made shoes and smelling of gentleman's eau-de-cologne. All those years in Germany – from the time when she had first met him at Marienbad, when she was seventeen and he thirty-six, right till 1938, when they had had to leave – he had always looked the same: small, bald, rosy-cheeked, fresh, elegant. Only in England had he suddenly become old and mostly worn his dressing-gown.

Mrs. Gottlob gave a big sigh, which heaved her overfed body with its ill-functioning glands: 'Yes, there we were all different people.' She thought of Gottlob's butcher-shop, where you got the finest liver-sausage in the whole of Gelsenkirchen, and sighed again. 'Still, here we all are, no bones broken, eh, Lumbik? That must be Else,' she said, as the door-bell rang again.

Tiny Else, as plump as she was short, came in, all breathless, her coat flying open, her grey bun half drooping out of its pins, an enormous old leather handbag tucked under her arm. 'See, again I am late,' she cried, 'what can I do? Always work work, rush rush, Else this, Else that – every day at five o'clock I feel like giving my notice.' She put

down the handbag and fumbled at her hair, while Mr.
Lumbik stood behind her and gallantly helped her out of
her coat. She gave him a suspicious look: 'Are you making a
joke of me again, you there, Lumbik?' but carried on again
immediately – 'Just think, today at half-past four she comes
to me: Else, one little work, this skirt to be shortened for a
very special customer. Mrs. Davis, I say to her, it is half-
past four. I am today invited for a birthday party in Swiss
Cottage at five-thirty sharp —'

'Enough of your blah-blah-blah,' Mrs. Gottlob inter-
rupted her, 'and at least wish something for the birthday
child.'

Else raised both her hands to her forehead: 'You see,
even that has completely gone out of my – wait, I have
brought a present!' She began to grabble in the vast interior
of her handbag and brought up wrong things like keys, a
bunch of safety-pins and a bottle of aspirin. Then she held
up a letter and cried, 'Oh I must tell you, what news!' It
had a German stamp. Sonia, who always got excited when
she saw letters with foreign stamps, cried, 'I hope good
news?'

'And what good news – my compensation! Ten thousand
marks!'

'Else, how nice!'

Mrs. Gottlob snatched the letter and read it. 'You should
have asked for twenty thousand,' she commented. She was
quite an expert on compensation. All her friends, all her
lodgers, had had compensation from Germany for their
losses; she herself had collected handsomely for the butcher-
shop. Of course, Sonia had had the most of all, for she and
her family had lost the most. Sonia was a rich woman again
now, which was as it should be.

'Ten thousand is also a nice little bit,' Else said, all red with pleasure. 'Now what shall I do with my ten thousand? I think perhaps first a nice holiday in Switzerland in a good hotel —'

'Oh Else, let's go to St. Moritz!' Sonia cried. She clapped her hands together, her eyes shone, her big body swayed on the slender, elegant legs. 'I was there with Papa and Mama in – when was it? Years and years ago, when I was fifteen. Oh it was so beautiful!'

'Na, and the birthday coffee?' Mrs. Gottlob reminded. Sonia went out into the kitchen, and soon she came back with the coffee-pot and they all sat round the table.

'So today is a good day for us all,' Mr. Lumbik said. 'First, there is someone's birthday.' And he languished across the table, so that Sonia became shy and peered down into her coffee cup, and Mrs. Gottlob gave him a sharp push and said, 'Keep your eyes to yourself, Lumbik.' He shut them immediately and sat up, prim and sheep-like, so that Sonia and Else burst out laughing like two schoolgirls. 'Always a success with the ladies,' he commented. 'So first this birthday. Then Miss Else gets her compensation and goes ski-ing in St. Moritz.'

'Yes,' cried Else, 'I will break my legs also for my ten thousand – we only live once, yu-hu!'

'And Karl Lumbik is made a British citizen, Class 4.'

'So,' said Mrs. Gottlob, her mouth full of *apfel strudel*, 'you are also one of us now.'

'That is just what she said to me when I got mine – that Mrs. Davis,' Else said. 'So you are one of us now, Else. Yes, I said, Mrs. Davis, I am one of you.' She gave a snort of contempt: 'I would rather tear out my arms and legs – "one of us"! If she opens her mouth, at once you know what class of people she comes from.' Else herself came from a very respectable family and never forgot what was due to

her. Her father, Emil Levy, had been a High School teacher
and a leading citizen of Schweinfurt; he had also, till the
Nazis came, been a very patriotic German and there had
always been a picture of the Kaiser and his family in the
Levy drawing-room.

Sonia said, 'English Jews are all so uncultured, they are
not like we were in Germany.'

'Uncultured!' Else cried. 'If you say to her Beethoven, she
will think you have said a bad word.'

'Do you know about Moyshe Rotblatt from Pinsk who was
taken to *Tristan und Isolde*?' Mr. Lumbik said.

'None of your kind of stories now, Lumbik,' Mrs. Gottlob
said. 'You are in good company.'

'The best company,' Mr. Lumbik said. 'Twenty years ago
if you had said to me, Karl Lumbik, in twenty years time
you will be drinking coffee with three very fine ladies in a
luxury flat, with central heating and lift —'

'Well, thank God, we are all a bit better off than we were
twenty years ago,' Else said.

'If only he had waited,' Sonia said. 'He never believed
things could be well again one day. I would say to him
"Otto, it is dark now but the sun will come again"; "no,"
he said, "it is all finished." He didn't want to live any more,
you see.'

'There were many days I also didn't want to live any
more,' Else said. 'After I had sat for ten hours at the back of
the shop, sewing my eyes out for Mrs. Davis, and then
come home to the furnished room where the bed wasn't
made and I couldn't find a shilling for the gas to heat up a
tin — I would say to myself, Else, what are you doing here?
Father, mother, sisters all gone, why are you still here,
finish off now.'

'Who hasn't had such days?' Mr. Lumbik said. 'But then

you go to the café, you play a game of chess, you hear a new joke, and everything is well again.' He smiled and somewhere a gold tooth twinkled so merrily, so bravely, that Sonia's heart quite leaped and she thought he is a good man.

Then Werner came home, and he said, 'Oh nice – a coffee-party.'

'What coffee-party?' Mrs. Gottlob said indignantly. 'It is a birthday-party.'

'Oh my God!' Werner said. He clapped his hand in front of his mouth and looked at his mother with large guilty eyes.

'So he has forgotten the mother's birthday!' Mrs. Gottlob cried.

'I thought only husbands forgot birthdays,' Mr. Lumbik said facetiously.

'What can I say?' Werner said to his mother.

'No no, what does it matter,' she said quickly.

'Of course it matters. It matters terribly.' He took both her hands and kissed her cheek with a slightly condescending affection. He was the same height as she was, a handsome boy with thick brown hair and an elegant air.

'No kissing now!' cried Mrs. Gottlob. 'You are a bad boy and should be smacked.'

'For one kiss from Werner, I also would forgive him everything,' Else said. Werner stooped down to kiss her cheek, saying, 'How are you, Tante Else?' She shut her eyes in rapture: 'Sonia, why do you have such a son?' Sonia looked on, smiling and proud.

'Sit down next to the old Gottlob now,' Mrs. Gottlob said, patting the seat beside her, 'and tell her all about your girl-friends.'

'Which one would you like to hear about?' said Werner, hitching up his well-creased trousers and crossing one leg over the other to display elegant socks. 'There's the blonde, then there's the brunette, and – my favourite – the red-head —'

'Mine come in only one colour,' said Mr. Lumbik. 'Grey.' But now that Werner was there, nobody listened to him.

Mrs. Gottlob shook her finger at Werner. 'You can't impress me. For me you will only be little Werner Wolff who comes running down the stairs to his Tante Gottlob's kitchen and says Tante Gottlob, bake a nice cheese-cake for me! Yes yes, now you pretend you have forgotten!' She pinched his cheek, a bit harder than he liked.

'Of course not, how can we ever forget?' Sonia said. She spoke in a hearty, grateful voice, though she would have preferred to forget the years in Mrs. Gottlob's house, the bed sitting-room where Otto shivered over the gas-fire and the noise of the other refugee lodgers quarrelling over whose turn it was next to use the bathroom.

'Werner,' Else cried, 'only think where we are going! To St. Moritz!'

'St. Moritz?' He lifted an eyebrow, smiled, looking charming. 'But Mutti must have been there, long ago, with Mama and Papa —'

'He is laughing at me!' Sonia wailed, stretching out a hand as if to defend herself. He caught it and kissed it and continued, 'That must have been the year after Karlsruhe, or was it the year after Bad Ems, when she had that lovely white-lace dress with a flower at her waist and played the piano by moonlight?'

'Well laugh then,' Sonia said, 'but they were beautiful times. Mama's health was delicate —'

'Of course,' Werner put in with mock solemnity.

'Shush now! And just think, Else, twice a year we would go for holidays, once in summer, once in winter, always to some very beautiful place where we lived in big hotels —'

'With red plush carpets and a winter garden and five o'clock tea *à l'anglaise*,' Werner said.

'All right!' Sonia cried, tossing her head in gay girlish defiance. 'So you laugh – but if we hadn't gone to Marienbad that year, where would you be now?' She looked round triumphantly, having made her forceful point.

Werner clasped his hands and swayed his head like a coy little girl. 'And whom did pretty Sonia Rothenstein, on holiday in Marienbad with Papa and Mama, whom did this well-bred, well-brought-up young lady meet in Marienbad?'

'Werner, today you are terrible,' said Sonia, glowing and happy.

'Yes yes, it is always like that,' Mrs. Gottlob said. 'They make fun of the parents.' She tried to pinch his cheek again, but he got it away in time.

'It is strange,' said Mr. Lumbik, still a few paces behind, 'I have stayed in so many hotels in my life but none has ever had a red plush carpet.'

'Tell more, Werner!' Else said. 'I want to hear the whole romance!' Her round cheeks were glowing – she had loved romance all her life and now, at spinster fifty, was as eager and waiting for it as ever.

'Else, why do you encourage him?' Sonia protested.

'But I must hear what it is like when a young lady goes on holiday to Marienbad. Perhaps shall we go to Marienbad instead of St. Moritz, Sonia? Who knows what will happen to us – you with your looks and me with my ten thousand? We have a fine chance!' She nudged Sonia's arm and screwed her apple-round face into an expression of bliss.

'I will tell you something else strange,' Mr. Lumbik said. 'You know, I have never been away on holiday.'

This time he was taken notice of: 'Never away on holiday!' cried Sonia and Else; and Mrs. Gottlob said, 'Is there another of your jokes coming, Lumbik?'

'Really, it is quite true. In Vienna, why should I go away on a holiday? My whole life was a holiday.'

'Yes yes, we know what kind of a holiday,' Mrs. Gottlob said.

'I had my friends there, my chess, my girl-friends, the café-houses, the opera – what should I want with a holiday?'

'How silly,' said Else. 'Everyone wants a summer holiday. Every year, when the schools were closed, my father took all six of us to the mountains and we stayed there in a Pension. It was called Pension Katz, I remember it so well.'

'And then afterwards —' He spread his hands and hunched his shoulders. 'A poor refugee tries to make a living, he doesn't make holidays. But all the same, I'm a much-travelled man – Budapest, Prague, Shanghai, Bombay, London, is that bad for one lifetime?'

'What sort of travelling is that?' said Mrs. Gottlob. 'That is only tramping.'

'It is true,' Mr. Lumbik admitted, 'some people travel for pleasure, for – how does one say?'

'For kicks,' Werner said.

'For kicks, thank you, and some travel because – yes, because they are kicked. Is this a bad pun, Mr. Werner? I am being very English now, for I am making puns so that I can apologize for them.'

'There is no need to boast, you there, Lumbik,' Else said. 'We have already heard how you are a British citizen now.'

'Yes, now I am a British citizen and no one can say to me

any more "Pack your bags, Lumbik! Time to move on."
It is so restful, it is quite bad for my nerves.'

'Well,' Werner said, lazily stretching his legs, 'it's time for
me now to do a bit of bag-packing.'

Sonia looked up with large anxious eyes: 'Werner, what
for?'

'I'm off to Rome soon,' and seeing his mother's face – 'oh
come on, darling, I told you I might be going.'

She lowered her eyes and clenched her large white hand
with the diamond ring in her lap. Mr. Lumbik looked at her
with compassion and tenderness. The others were looking at
Werner.

'How exciting, Werner!' Else said. 'Why are you going?'

'There are things doing there – and I'm tired of London.
So, pack your bags, Werner! Time to move on.' He smiled
his handsome smile at Mr. Lumbik who, however, did not
respond.

'So it's not good enough for you with the mother any
more,' Mrs. Gottlob scolded. 'This lovely flat, the beautiful
meals she cooks for you – you leave it all and say good-
bye.'

'What will you do there, Werner?' Sonia said in a small
voice.

'I told you – there's lots doing there, films and, oh lots.
Don't worry, darling,' he said, trying to sound light and gay,
but with an edge of exasperation all the same.

'Of course I don't worry,' she said quickly. There wasn't
any need to worry. There was enough money now and he
could do in Rome what he did in London – a little film-work
here, a little art-photography there, a lot of parties, a lot of
girl-friends.

He looked at his watch. 'Heavens, I must fly! I've got a
date at seven!' He disappeared into his own room which

adjoined his mother's. The moment he had gone, Sonia began to cry.

'Sonia, *liebchen!*' Else cried. Mrs. Gottlob clicked her tongue and said in her rough way, 'Na, what is this?'

'How silly I am,' Sonia sobbed. Mr. Lumbik looked tactfully at a picture on the wall showing Sonia's parents honeymooning in Biarritz.

'You see, I keep thinking how different it would have been,' Sonia said, wiping at her eyes with her little handkerchief. 'Otto would have retired by now and Werner would be running the factory. He would be Werner Wolff, Director of SIGBO, everybody would know and respect him —'

'So who respects me here!' Else cried. 'For Mrs. Davis I am only her alteration hand, but I know I am still Else Levy, daughter of Oberlehrer Levy of Schweinfurt, so what does it matter to me what Mrs. Davis thinks?'

'But the children,' Sonia said. 'We know who we are, but what does my Werner know, and my Lilo?' At the thought of Lilo, new tears came and she clasped the handkerchief to her eyes. 'My poor Lilo – I have had such a lovely girlhood, such lovely dresses and always parties and dancing-classes and the Konservatorium in Berlin for my piano-playing. And she has had only hard work in the Kibbutz, hard work with her hands, and those horrible white blouses and shorts —' Her voice broke and she said, 'My handkerchief is quite wet.'

'The birthday present!' cried Else, snatching her large leather bag. She fumbled inside and this time came up with three lace-trimmed handkerchiefs. 'Happy birthday, Sonia, it is very good lace.'

'Oh Else, how beautiful,' Sonia said gratefully and immediately used one to wipe her eyes.

'You see, it is a very useful present,' Else said. 'But next time it is only for blowing the nose – no more tears, understand?' she said strictly.

'And I would like to know what cause for tears you have,' Mrs. Gottlob said. 'You are alive, you are healthy, the children are alive and healthy, what else matters?'

'You know sometimes I say to myself,' Mr. Lumbik said, 'Lumbik, what have you achieved in your life? And then I answer myself I have survived, I am still alive, and this is already a success story.'

'For once this Lumbik has also something sensible to say!' Mrs. Gottlob said. 'Be grateful to God for still letting you be here, Mrs. Wolff, and let your Werner and Lilo look after themselves.'

'One thing I have been asking and asking myself,' Mr. Lumbik said. 'For me it is a very serious question: shall I be offered some more *apfel strudel* or no?'

'Always thinking of the stomach, Lumbik,' Mrs. Gottlob said. 'Na, perhaps another cup of coffee will also do us good.'

'We will start celebrating the birthday all over again!' Else cried. 'Birthday-parties are so nice, and today we'll have two!'

'For such a special birthday child,' Mr. Lumbik said in his tender voice, 'even two isn't enough.'

'Ach Mr. Lumbik,' Sonia said reproachfully, blushing.

He held up one entreating little finger: 'Remember my birthday wish from you!'

'Karl,' she said, pouring coffee with a smiling, averted face.

'This is something new now,' said Mrs. Gottlob, and Else gave Mr. Lumbik's arm a pinch and said, 'You have been making sheep's eyes at Sonia long enough – now it is my turn, I am also a nice young lady.'

'You are all three nice young ladies,' said Mr. Lumbik, and this compliment made Mrs. Gottlob laugh so much that she went quite red and had a cramp in her throat.

When Werner came out of his room, dressed for his date, he found them having a very merry party. 'Well, I'm off,' he said, but no one heard him. Mr. Lumbik was telling a story about his experiences in Shanghai. ''Bye!' called Werner. Only Sonia glanced at him. 'Are you going, Werner?' she said in an absent-minded way as she poured another cup of coffee for Mr. Lumbik. Werner smiled at their preoccupation; he was glad to see them having a good time.

LIKE BIRDS, LIKE FISHES

RAJ had come to the city with high hopes, but they had been disappointed. It was, after all, not much different from what it had been at home. He lived with his brother Shankar, who was much older than he was and had a family of five children, the eldest of whom was only a few years younger than Raj. This boy – whose pet-name was Munna – was Raj's only companion, and they went for walks together and, when they had money, to the cinema. Munna was still studying, so he never had any money at all; and Raj had very little, for his brother always took charge of his monthly salary, deducting some for Raj's keep and some for sending home to their mother; after which there was not much left.

Raj worked all day behind the counter of a dry-cleaner's shop. The owner of the shop was a distant relative and that was how Raj had got the job. But he did not like it. The shop was only a little cubicle with nothing in it except a counter and a cupboard in which Raj hung up the clothes which came back cleaned from the workshop. He was alone in the shop all day, and when customers came he had to examine the clothes they brought and write down details and give a receipt. But not many customers came, for it was a shabby little shop with no attempt at any modern decoration. Most people preferred to go to *Rite-Wite* opposite, which was very smart with neon-lighting and a cardboard figure of a pretty woman in the window and a radio which played all day.

At night he was supposed to be attending classes in a

college. He did not go very often, for not only did he find
these classes dull but he was also tired at night and did not
feel like improving himself. It was his brother Shankar who
always urged him on to improve himself and, of course, his
mother expected it too, and his whole family. They all
wanted him to pass some examination, so that he could become a government servant, like Shankar, and get a secure
post in a Ministry with pension and provident fund. Altogether he was expected to become exactly like his brother,
who was thought to have done very well for himself; the
brother thought so too and always held himself up as an
example to Raj. But Raj was not convinced. It was true,
Shankar was a regular government servant and brought
home a regular salary, but nevertheless he could very
seldom afford to go to a cinema or buy any new clothes, and
towards the end of the month his wife often had to borrow
tea and sugar from the neighbours.

They lived in a government quarter, which was a tiny
yellow house with barred windows joined on to identical
other tiny yellow houses in long rows like barracks. One
day their neighbours were transferred to the South, and the
next day a new family moved in. When Raj came home
from the dry-cleaner's, he found a girl standing outside the
house next door. She had her back to the street and was
leaning with her head buried against the wall of the house,
and she was crying. At first Raj wanted to hurry on and
pretend he had not noticed, but there was something very
appealing in the way she stood there, so slender and
unhappy with a long plait hanging down her back and going
up and down as she cried. He cleared his throat a few times
and called to her, 'Are you ill?'

She went on crying, but after a while she uncovered her
face and had a look at him. He liked her face and was glad

it was not as tear-stained as he had feared. She looked at him quite carefully and then she walked into the house. She was thin, but her hips were nicely developed and went from side to side as she walked.

She called from inside, 'You can come in, if you like.' When he did so, he found the room had not been arranged at all and there were only some chairs and two string-cots standing upright, and a few trunks and bundles. She stood in the middle of these things, wringing her hands: 'It is such an ugly house.' She kicked at the floor and said in a contemptuous, tearful voice, 'A cement floor! In our house we always had marble chips!'

'I live next door,' he said, as if to comfort her with that.

'And no flush.' She sank down on one of the bundles and buried her face in her hands. 'Please go away.'

Raj found he did not want to do so at all. To prolong the conversation, he said, 'Where are your father and mother?'

She looked up and, instead of crying, she was laughing. 'But I live with my husband!'

Raj was suddenly shy: he had thought she was the daughter of the house and now he found she was the wife, a married woman. She laughed some more and got up and pranced round the room with her hands on her hips: 'Yes, I am a married woman, so I hope you will be very respectful to me.' She stopped in front of him and had another good look at him. 'How old are you?'

'Nineteen,' he said miserably.

'And I am only seventeen, but I have already been married three months. Would you like to see some of my wedding presents?' She begun to untie one of the bundles and brought out a lamp which consisted of a naked woman with a dog at her feet and holding up a tasselled orange shade. 'It was given by my elder sister,' she said. 'She is married to a very rich man, a film distributor.' She drew out some more things – three ivory elephants walking over a bridge, an electric kettle, a silver toast-rack. Raj was very much impressed.

'But where to put these things in such an ugly house!' she cried.

'Perhaps you should unpack and arrange everything?' But she seemed too despondent to do so. He felt a strong desire to help her.

Soon he was pushing the beds into the next room and distributing the chairs and a little table in as attractive a manner as he could. She stayed sitting on the floor and did not look at him while he was arranging everything, though she let him do just as he wished. She did not talk to him either, except once to ask him his name and to tell him that hers was Nilima; which he thought was a pretty name and suited her.

When he had finished, he looked round and was pleased with the effect. The room was a little bare perhaps, and the walls and ceiling had not been whitewashed too well, but her wedding presents looked very splendid. He glanced down at her, but her lower lip was pushed out and two tears fell from her eyes. 'If you had seen my parents' house . . . We had a sofa-set in blue and silver, and there were curtains in front of all the windows.'

Raj felt ashamed and as if it were his fault that things were not nicer.

When he got home, the first thing he did was take out his prayer book and count the money he kept inside it, tied up in a handkerchief. He always counted his money when he felt disturbed or depressed. It was a great comfort. There were 63 rupees now, mostly in soiled and tattered one- or two-rupee notes, which he had saved by not buying any cold drinks or betel and frequently walking the six miles and back to his work. He had no very clear idea of what he wanted to do with the money; but the thought of it was always mixed up with thoughts of his friend Dev, who had run away from home and from the job his family had found for him. All sorts of rumours had been heard about Dev and the adventurous life he was leading. Once he was a guide at the Ajanta caves, and another time he was selling coloured pictures of gods and saints at fairs and festivals. He ate anything anywhere and lost caste over and over again, but it seemed he was happy, travelling from one end of the country to the other and doing whatever he liked. The last that was heard of him he had become a sadhu and had shaved his head and wore an orange robe. Once Raj had received a postcard from him. It read: 'Like birds, like fishes, so man also,' and though Raj could not quite fathom the meaning of this message, he felt himself deeply moved by it.

He did not meet Nilima again for some time, but he thought about her quite often. He would have liked to know a lot more about her. Sometimes he asked his sister-in-law, casually, 'There are new people next door? What are they like?' But even she could not give him any information – which was surprising, for if there was one person who could usually be relied upon to know all about her neighbours, it was Mrs. Shankar. She was a cheerful, sociable woman, with steel-framed spectacles slightly askew and big protruding teeth which made her look as if she was smiling all the time. She spent a good deal of her day walking round the colony, drinking tea and having pleasant chats with her friends, and consequently she was always too busy to dress properly or do her hair. Her house too was not as neat and clean as it might have been – though just before her husband came home in the evenings, she always did some very hurried tidying up, aided by her eldest daughter, both of them nervous and giggling and like two schoolgirls afraid to be caught.

Mrs. Shankar and her friends were very disappointed in the new neighbour. Not only did she refuse to talk to them but, worse, no one seemed to be able to find out anything about her – what sort of family she came from and how much her father earned and what dowry had been given with her at her marriage. Of course, they were sure that sooner or later someone would turn up who had been to Nilima's home-town and knew all about her family; but meanwhile it was frustrating to have her there and know nothing about her. 'She won't even let you into the house,' Mrs. Shankar complained to Raj. 'When you knock at the door, she opens it a little bit and then she says she is resting. Is that the behaviour of a neighbour?' Raj felt tempted to boast to her that he, at any rate, had been allowed inside and that he had arranged her things for her and been shown her wedding presents. But he restrained himself; he had not told anyone about that, not even Munna.

He always looked hopefully towards her house when he passed it, but she was never to be seen. When he went walking with Munna, he contrived to go very slowly outside her house and talk and laugh rather loudly, leaning with his elbow on Munna's shoulder in a debonair manner. Munna never noticed these tactics; only sometimes he asked, 'Why are you going so slowly? Let us hurry, it is time for our meal.'

At last what Raj had hoped for happened, and she appeared at her door while he was passing with Munna. She

called to him, 'You can come and listen to my radio, if you
like.' Munna was very much surprised, he looked round to
see whom she might be talking to. But Raj pulled him into
the house.

The room was exactly as he had arranged it, except that
there were a few clothes lying about and a half-drunk cup
of tea and an open cardboard box of sweetmeats on a chair.
A transistor radio was playing western dance-music. Munna
looked at the radio and his eyes and mouth grew round:
'How small it is!'

'Perhaps it is small,' Nilima said, 'but you can get all the
stations in the world on it. Ceylon, China, England . . .'
Munna went close and looked at it with awe and admiration.

Nilima sat on the floor by the chair on which the sweetmeats stood and began to eat them. In between she said,
'This is such a horrible place to live, and what is worst is
that there is no one to talk with.'

Raj wanted to ask what about your husband? But he saw
that it would be an indelicate question.

However, she talked about him of her own accord. She
said, with a sigh, 'He is all day in the office and at night
there are classes to attend. He wants very much to improve
himself.' Raj thought of his own classes where he too ought
to have been improving himself.

'Of course,' Nilima said, 'he must improve himself – my
goodness, I am not going to stay here for ever, he must get
promoted quickly and then we will move to a better house
where nicer people will be living.'

'I also attend evening classes,' Raj said. 'Soon I hope to
get a very good post in government service.'

'You should have seen what it was like in my house!
Every day people came to visit us, rich people in cars, and

there were parties – If you turn the knob,' she told Munna, who was still gazing at the radio, 'you will get all the different stations from the whole world.'

Raj said, 'At Diwali time the Residents Association of these quarters give a party. There is a big tent and a lot to eat and also a programme of song and dance.'

Nilima looked contemptuous; she ate another sweetmeat and when she had finished chewing it, she said, 'Thank you, such dull parties are no enjoyment for me.'

'They are not dull,' Raj said with spirit.

'If you had seen the parties in my home – oh,' she said, suddenly disgusted, 'what do you know about parties or about anything at all?' She took another sweetmeat and ate it in an angry way.

Raj too was angry and he was about to say something suitable in reply, when Munna held up one finger and said, 'Listen!' The radio was crackling in a strange language.

'It is Chinese,' Nilima said.

Raj said, 'No, it is Russian.'

She forced a laugh: 'What ignorance, not to be able to tell the difference between Russian and Chinese.'

'It *is* Russian!'

'Please don't shout in my house.'

Raj jerked his head towards the door and said to Munna, 'Come on, we are going.'

Nilima gave a little push to the box of sweetmeats: 'You can eat one, if you like' – though there were only a few left and those not very good ones. 'Do you play cards? We could have a game of cards.'

Raj walked out of the door, with Munna trailing reluctantly behind.

She called after them, 'You can come tomorrow and play cards with me!' Munna gave Raj a nudge. 'I invite you to come!' she called. Raj, swaggering off with his hands in his pockets, just turned his head a little bit to say over his shoulder, 'I shall probably be too busy.'

Next day he went to his classes. It was very dull and he was not really listening to the teacher, but he stuck it out till the end. On his way home he walked past Nilima's house rather quickly and did not even glance in that direction. And the next day he went to his classes again, and the next, and behaved altogether in an exemplary manner. But the evening after that when he came home, he found she had come to visit and was enjoying a cup of tea with Mrs. Shankar. She was sitting in Shankar's rocking-chair, gently rocking herself to and fro.

'My sister also lives in very good style,' she was saying. 'Her husband has an income of 2,000 rupees a month.'

Mrs. Shankar clasped her hands: '2,000 rupees!' She nudged Raj, 'You hear?' and she laughed with pleasure at the thought of someone else's wealth. Raj stared steadfastly at his brother's framed B.A. certificate on the wall.

'Only my fate has not been so good,' Nilima sighed and rocked herself to and fro in a melancholy way.

Mrs. Shankar at once began to sigh with her: 'What to do? The lot of one is cast in the sun, that of another in the shade. It is so in life.' She looked mournful, out of compassion with all those (including perhaps herself) whose lot had been cast in the shade.

Nilima stopped rocking and said in a proud voice: 'Of course, after a few years he will reach very high position, and then it will be very different for us.'

And Mrs. Shankar looked happy with her, she beamed through her spectacles and smiled with her big protruding teeth; though, as far as she herself was concerned, there was not much chance of anything ever being different.

But Raj was frowning. He didn't like to hear Nilima talk like that. Perhaps he didn't like to think of her soaring away into higher regions, and the rest of them all left behind to be as they always had been.

She noticed his displeasure, and she pointed at him and said, 'I think he is a very bad-tempered boy!' and then she laughed in an affected way.

'Oh no,' Mrs. Shankar said, 'he is a good boy.'

'I shall go away,' Nilima said and she really got up. 'I think he doesn't like me to stay.'

Mrs. Shankar began to protest, but Nilima went out. Raj followed her.

'Why didn't you come when I invited you?' she said.

'In the evenings I am always busy.'

'What lies.'

Mrs. Shankar stood smiling in the doorway and called, 'Please come tomorrow also! Come every day!'

Nilima pulled a comical face: 'How she talks – she is so stupid and ugly.' To Raj she said, 'I feel very bored in the evenings when he is gone to classes.' She looked at him and then at once she lowered her eyes away from him and glanced down and arranged the folds of her sari to fall prettily over her foot: 'Please come,' she said.

So next day he did not go to his classes. Instead he went straight home where he polished his shoes and combed his hair with oil. He said nothing to Munna but went quietly next door. Nilima had some cards laid out and she also had a new box of sweetmeats and the radio was on rather loudly, playing love-songs from the latest films. They had a game of rummy. Nilima played with great concentration, showing the tip of her tongue between her teeth, and when she won, she laughed and bobbed up and down in her seat, but when she lost, she was very miserable as if something tragic had happened to her. They played for some time, till they got tired of the game, and then they ate sweetmeats and talked about all sorts of things.

He did not go to his classes again. Sometimes he did not even bother to go home, but went straight to Nilima's house. It was a little awkward to go home, for if his brother saw him, he would always ask him, 'Why haven't you gone to your classes?' Then he had to make up some excuse, such as that the college was closed out of respect for the Principal's mother who had died. Even so his brother gave him a lecture on how he had to study hard so that he could get a good job in government service and be married and become a householder like Shankar himself. There was a framed text on the wall which had *Home Sweet Home* embroidered in red cross-stitch on a blue background. Shankar had bought it second-hand in the Thieves' Bazaar for Rs.1.50, and it served not only to hide a patch of damp on the wall but also as a symbol and figurehead for the life of the Shankar family. Shankar often pointed at it and said, 'There is my proudest achievement of all! A happy home, a contented family – with such a man becomes a king.' Mrs. Shankar always looked on such occasions as if she wanted to laugh, but of course she didn't, instead she put on a very serious expression and nodded her head up and down.

It was quite different in Nilima's house. Here no one talked about Raj's classes or his duty in life. Instead he talked himself – about his grandmother, of whom he had been very fond and who had told him many stories out of the *Mahabharata* and all the other old books; how at home he had sometimes gone boating on the river with friends; about the 63 rupees he had saved and kept in his prayer book; and about his friend Dev who had run away and had become a sadhu. He was not always sure that Nilima was listening to him, but he talked all the same. She sat either on the floor or sometimes on a chair with her feet drawn up on its seat and playing with her toes. He became very familiar with the way she turned her head and with the nape of her neck, which had a little film of hair reaching right down into her back. Sometimes she stroked her cheek or her arm very slowly and thoughtfully, as if to feel how soft the skin was. Her husband was never there. Raj was surprised at this absence; he thought that if he were married to a wife like Nilima, he would probably want to be with her as much as he could.

Sometimes Munna came too. He was really no trouble at all, but always sat quite happily with the radio and tried to get all the different stations. He showed no interest in their conversation, but it seemed that he took more notice of Nilima than he usually did of girls; for once at night, when they were together in the bed they shared, he whispered to Raj, 'If she were not so thin, she would be quite nice.'

One evening, as Raj and Nilima sat playing rummy and Munna was busy with the radio, Nilima's husband came in. He was small and thin and wore large spectacles with thick brown rims, which made him look like a schoolboy dressed up to appear like someone much older and cleverer. He expressed no surprise at the presence of Raj and Munna, but showed great interest in the card-game. He at once sat down and played with them. He won every game. He played at enormous speed and would not give them time to arrange their cards properly or to think which card to play next. He told Munna to turn off the radio because he could not concentrate with the noise. After every game he allowed himself a small smile and at once gathered up the cards again and shuffled them very skilfully. Raj wished they could stop and Nilima looked as if she wanted to cry; and at last she did cry and flung down her cards and said she wasn't playing any more. Her husband told Raj, 'Only you and I will play.' They did so, and of course Raj kept on losing. He became very hot and flushed, and he too felt like crying. Nilima and Munna yawned, but the husband kept on playing with great skill and smiling his small smile after each game. At last he had had enough, he pushed the cards together into a neat pile, placed them in their box and said, 'If you play with me more often, you might one day learn a good game.'

Mrs. Shankar was waiting for them in a state of great excitement. 'Her father is in jail,' she said in a sort of reverent whisper.

'What?' Raj said.

'In *jail*,' she said, still in a whisper but stretching her mouth wide in order to enunciate clearly.

It was a more interesting story than one usually heard about people. Nilima's father had been an ordinary clerk, but in a division dealing with import licences. He was thus in a position to show favour to a great number of wealthy businessmen and be shown favour to in return. He built a house for himself, bought a refrigerator and a radio, and dressed his wife and daughters in silk. He also placed his sons in profitable jobs and arranged very good matches for his daughters. But all this was too high a horse for such as he. Rumour and outraged gossip swirled around his beautiful new house and his silk-clad women; even the wedding-guests invited to participate in his daughters' splendid marriage-feasts furtively whispered together in groups. Neither he nor his family ever noticed anything: they were too busy enjoying themselves. But when at last the rumours penetrated into official quarters, he was suspended and an inquiry begun. By the time a case was made out and brought into court, only one daughter, Nilima, was left unmarried, and something had to be done about her rather quickly. A bridegroom was found and the wedding hurried through. It was the end of the father's money and he made what show he could with it, so that Nilima's wedding – though nothing compared with those of her sisters – was still of some consequence and certainly sufficed to astonish the bridegroom and his very ordinary family. The father was still there to take part in the festivities, but it was his second last public appearance. The last came a few days later, in court, to hear himself sentenced.

Shankar had only one comment to make on this story: 'Honesty,' he said, 'is the best policy,' and then he looked sternly at Raj and Munna and repeated the lesson to make sure it had been properly received. 'Remember that, boys, and your path in life is assured.' Munna looked virtuous and attentive, but Raj was busy chasing away flies that had settled on the sugar.

Yet he too was deeply impressed by this new information about Nilima. When she boasted in her usual way about what it had been like in her father's house, he was uncomfortable and felt ashamed for her. He was further exacerbated by Munna whose imagination had been caught by the idea of her father in jail. 'What do you think they get to eat in jail? Have they shaved his head? Are his legs chained?' It was a subject that fascinated Munna and he kept staring at Nilima in fascination too, as if to get some clearer image of her father (chained and shaved) through her. But she behaved as if nothing like that had ever happened. Though she often complained about her present situation, she had nothing but nostalgia for her past. How often, in the middle of a game, she suddenly flung down her cards and yawned and complained about how dull everything was! And then she recalled some particularly pleasant incident from her home-life – some picnic they had all gone to near a lake, everything they had eaten and the games they had played, the songs they had sung, the carriages with red-leather seats and horses with plumed bridles that had taken them there.

She hardly ever mentioned her husband. Only sometimes, when she was losing at cards, she nodded her head knowingly and said yes, it was easy for Raj to win over her, a simple young girl, but just let him try his skill against her husband, that would be a different story. Raj did his best to remain calm and merely shuffled and dealt again. But she was never satisfied till she had provoked him. She would go on to say how clever her husband was, how hard he worked, how quickly he would be promoted, how he would become rich and important and she with him, whereas Raj – she pushed out her lower lip in a way he already knew well: 'You are even too lazy to go to your evening-classes! All you will ever be is a clerk in your dry-cleaner's!' She watched him under lowered lids while she said all this and giggled to herself. But if he got angry and threw down his cards and made to go away, she would jump up and run after him; she caught his sleeve and implored, 'But it was only a joke, only a joke to make you laugh!' And she laughed, to demonstrate how, though at the same time her eyes were anxious, and, if he shook her off, then they filled with tears, and often she would throw herself to her knees and press her face into a chair and sob from out of there, 'If you go away, who else is there left to talk with me?' Munna's attention was diverted from the radio and he looked at her in astonishment and from her at Raj, reproachfully; and he began to fear that there would now be a big quarrel so that they would never be able to come again and his pleasant evenings would be at an end. But this never happened : even if there was a quarrel, and however angry Raj got, next evening they were always back again.

Once they found a taxi standing outside her door. They were surprised, and when they went in, they found her with a stout woman who she said was her sister from Bombay, married to a film distributor. The sister looked at them with mistrust : it was clear to her at once that they were very much beneath her in social and financial standing. She was some ten years older than Nilima, with a fat healthy face and a fat neck; she wore a sari of very bright-green silk, big gold ear-rings and rows of gold bangles on both her arms. She and Nilima were drinking some highly-coloured sherbet and they were busy over the contents of a box of jewels. Nilima drew out ear-rings, bracelets and a necklace and tried them on and looked into a mirror, smiling at herself and turning this way and that, while the sister watched with her hands folded over her stomach. Raj and Munna hovered by the door, and Munna looked longingly at the sherbet the two sisters were drinking. Nilima was very lively and kept on talking; once she glanced at them and said, 'Today I am too busy to play cards with you,' and then she went back to her conversation. The sister too glanced at Raj and Munna, in the same way as she had done when they first came in, and she said, 'They play cards with you?'

Nilima laughed. 'It is such a terrible place – you don't know, there is no one, no one to talk with, nothing to do.' The sister shook her head and gave another scathing look at Raj and Munna. 'You had better go away!' Nilima called to them. 'You can see, today my sister has come and we have many things to talk.'

Raj made furious resolutions, but nevertheless he was back again the next day. And Nilima took it for granted that he should be: everything was as before and Munna was allowed to listen to the radio again. She told them all about her sister – how much her husband earned a month and what sort of people she knew, the places she went to, the clothes she wore. Raj thought of the fat sister and the way she had looked at him.

Nilima said, 'Next month I shall go and stay with my sister in Bombay, and then what a good time I shall have!' She stretched her arms and clasped her hands above her head and laughed in anticipation. 'If I have a little time to spare' – and she looked at him sideways with bright, gay eyes – 'I shall think of you and feel sorry for you.'

Suddenly Raj said, 'And your father? You will think of him also?' Munna looked up startled from the radio.

Nilima said in a brave though shaking little voice, 'Why my father?'

Raj remembered the way she and her sister had drunk sherbet and gloated over the jewel-box. He said, 'Everybody knows,' in a cruel, contemptuous tone.

'What is there to know? It is not a shameful thing! In our country everybody has gone to jail – Gandhiji himself —'

Munna leaned forward eagerly: 'What do they get to eat in jail?'

'And Panditji also!'

'For bribery and corruption?' Raj said.

'It is an honour! Only people who have been in jail can hold high position!'

Just then Nilima's husband came in. He looked pleased when he saw the cards on the table and rubbed his hands: 'Come, I will teach you how to play a good game.'

Nilima picked up the cards and threw them in his direction, so that they scattered over the floor. Her husband adjusted his big spectacles on his small nose and cleared his throat in embarrassment. He looked at Raj as if for help. Munna began to pick up the cards, crawling all over the floor to do so.

'Today my classes finished early,' the husband explained to Raj. 'I have brought some files home —' he was carrying them in his hand and now he held them up like an alibi. 'Urgent work,' he said and again adjusted his spectacles.

'I am proud of my father and where he is!' Nilima said.

'Sh,' said her husband.

She stamped her foot. 'I *am* proud!' Munna gingerly picked up a card which had fallen near her feet. 'There is nothing to be ashamed of!'

Her husband gave a furtive look at Raj. 'There are people who don't understand, that is why it is better not to —'

'You are thinking only of what they will say in your office! You are afraid they will find out and stop your promotion! That is all you can ever think of – your promotion!'

Munna asked shyly, 'Are people in jail allowed to receive visitors?'

'You can be promoted and promoted, but you will never earn even half the money that my father earned. None of you will ever be like my father!'

'A clerk, Grade 3,' the husband sneered.

'There is nothing wrong in being a clerk, Grade 3,' Raj said. He had not expected to speak, but now that he had started, he grew heated and went on: 'What is wrong is to think always of money and position, and who is better and who is worse, that is wrong.'

'I see you are an anti-materialist philosopher,' the husband said. Raj did not know what this meant but he felt a desire to snatch off the other's spectacles and stamp on them.

Nilima said, 'Just because you know long words, you think you are very great.' Both she and Raj were glaring angrily at her husband.

'You will see how far I will go,' the husband said with a smile which did not look like a smile at all because most of his face remained so serious. Raj and Nilima both looked away from him simultaneously and their eyes met; Raj realized that he and she were on the same side. There was a short silence.

Then Nilima shouted at Raj, 'Why don't you go home? Who asked you to come here day after day and disturb me?'

But he knew that he would go back, again and again, and that she expected him to. He thought of her all the time now, and he made many plans. These did not include going to his classes or staying in his job at the dry-cleaner's. He thought of his friend Dev who had left everything and gone wherever he pleased; and then of Nilima and himself doing the same. There were so many far-away places where one could go and need never look back again, but just be free and happy like birds and fishes.

How little free and happy he was himself was brought home to him one evening, when he was about to leave for Nilima's house. His brother came home; he looked stern and displeased and said at once, 'Why are you not at your classes?'

'The Principal's mother has died.'

'She died many weeks ago.'

'Now they are carrying her ashes to Hardwar.' But he

saw that his brother was displeased not only about the college, but about something else as well.

Suddenly Shankar shouted, 'I hear you and Munna have been going to the neighbour's house!' As soon as they heard their father raise his voice, the younger children ran outside and from that safe distance looked in through the barred window.

Munna was frightened. He said, 'They have a radio, we have been listening —'

'When the husband is not at home!' Shankar thundered. His wife came running in from the kitchen. She had been kneading dough and it stuck to her hands so that she had to hold them extended.

'That is the story I have to hear in the office!' He caught Munna's ear and began to twist it; Munna squealed and begged for pardon, while his brothers and sisters looked in, solemn and silent, from outside the window.

'They have been playing cards,' Mrs. Shankar said. 'It is nothing, no harm.' She bit her lip and looked tearful, but did not know what to say further to appease her husband.

'People have been talking – about *my* family. What is my position as a government officer? Answer me!' he shouted, giving a really vicious twist to Munna's ear, so that both Munna and his mother let out a loud cry.

'Leave him alone,' Raj said – almost ordered, as if it was he who was the elder brother. Everyone looked at him in amazement, including Shankar, who was so startled that he let go of Munna's ear. When he had recovered sufficiently, he grew more furious than ever and made at once for Raj with his hand uplifted. But when he got within striking range, his hand sank back again and he contented himself with shouting.

Raj turned away and went into the little room where he slept at night with Munna and the other children. He took his clothes from the shelf and his other pair of shoes. His sister-in-law followed him and asked, 'What are you doing?' in an anxious, frightened voice. Shankar was still shouting in the next room; he was shouting about honour, respectability and family tradition to an attentive audience of Munna and the other children, who remained safely outside the window.

Raj put his things into his battered cardboard case, and then he rolled up his bedding. Mrs. Shankar said, 'Where can you go?' imploringly. Last of all he took his 63 rupees tied in a handkerchief out of his prayer book. The Prayer Book he left behind. Mrs. Shankar said, 'You will starve – you will have to beg from people in the streets.'

'The sanctity of the home must be respected first and foremost!' Shankar was shouting in the next room.

Raj tied string round his case to fasten it. Mrs. Shankar helped him, putting her finger on the knot he made, and at the same time she said, 'Everyone sometimes feels like running away, but it is not so easy.' He hoisted his roll of bedding on to his shoulder and she helped him steady it. 'One must eat also,' she said, 'and have somewhere to sleep and live.'

He passed into the next room. Shankar was still telling the children about morals, tradition and the honour of a government servant. When he saw Raj with his bedding on his shoulder, he cried, 'I forbid you! I forbid you to leave this house!' It was evident from the bluster in his voice that he did not expect to be taken notice of.

Nilima was also surprised to see Raj with his luggage. But soon she was very excited and it did not take her long to decide to pack up her own things too. She had a very nice strong suitcase, with a proper lock and a key to it, into which she hastily flung her saris and jewels. All the time she was packing, she kept on talking. 'Let us go to Agra first – we shall see the Taj Mahal and many other beautiful buildings.' She told him how once her father had taken the whole family to Agra and they had eaten some wonderful pilao in a hotel and had bought a marble replica of the Taj Mahal which could be lit up with a bulb from inside. Her suitcase would not shut, so Raj had to take everything out again and pack it properly, and then it shut quite easily. 'And from Agra we can go to Jaipur, I have a cousin living there who will be very happy to see me.' Just as Raj had finally locked the suitcase, someone came to the door. It was Munna.

He held out a carefully folded five-rupee note: 'Mama sent this for you.' He looked at their packed cases and said, 'Please take me also.'

'Go home,' Raj said.

A big tear rolled down Munna's cheek.

Nilima suddenly seized her radio and she thrust it into Munna's arms: 'You can keep it, if you like.' His whole expression changed at once. He stood holding the radio as if it were a bomb that would explode in his hands and blow him up with happiness.

Raj looked round him. He saw the lamp, which had been Nilima's wedding-present from her sister, and he unplugged it and piled it into Munna's arms on top of the radio. 'For your mother,' he said.

Nilima went round the room, collecting her other wedding-presents. The three elephants walking over the bridge, the electric kettle, the silver toast-rack – everything was given to Munna. He had to sit down to be able to hold everything; he was completely covered with gifts.

.   .   .   .   .   .

At the station Raj bought two third-class tickets, one way only. Nilima was more excited than ever, for the station was crowded and people came and went with rolls of bedding and cloth bundles and big earthenware jugs of drinking-water. She said she loved travelling, she loved stations and engines. There were men with barrows selling coloured drinks and cream-horns and magazines and plaster-busts of gods. She wanted to buy everything: she said she was hungry, and thirsty, and now that she had given away all her wedding-presents, she would like to have a plaster bust of Krishna and Radha; and certainly she must have something to read on the train, otherwise she would be very bored. He bought her two film-magazines and had to change the five-rupee note sent for him by his sister-in-law.

There was still half an hour before the train to Agra was to leave, but the third-class compartment was already very crowded. All the benches were taken, and people squatted on the floor and hung out from the door. 'No room!' they shouted, but Raj forced his way through and found a corner where Nilima could sit down on her suitcase. It was very hot in the carriage and there was a strong smell of poor people and of the lavatories which had not been cleaned very well. The passengers were still disputing their places with each other and several quarrels were going on. But Raj felt secure in their corner; he thought of how tomorrow he would not have to go to the dry-cleaner's nor come home to his brother's house for his meal. He glanced down at Nilima and was shocked to see that she was crying.

He bent down and whispered, 'Are you ill?'

She cried quietly to herself. In between she said, 'When my father took us travelling, we always went first-class and had a compartment all to ourselves.'

'It is only for a few hours.'

After a while she said, 'I want to go home.' She said it quite loudly, so that people began to look at them both. 'Take me home!' she said, even louder.

'I can go and change our tickets for second-class.'

'I want to go home to my husband!'

People now looked indignantly at Raj. Some of them said, 'Perhaps it is an abduction case.'

Nilima got up from her suitcase. She said to the passengers standing all round, 'Let me through, I want to go back to my husband.' People pushed each other out of the way and a passage was formed for her to get out again. She walked down the carriage and Raj followed with her suitcase. Everyone was very interested in them and those who had been quarrelling stopped doing so and discussed this unusual incident instead.

Raj, walking behind her with her suitcase, kept on saying, 'I can get second-class tickets.' She did not turn round. When they got to the door, she jumped off but he stayed behind and handed her suitcase down to her. The people in the carriage all crowded round the door behind Raj and those who could not get a place rushed to the windows and stuck their heads through the bars. They explained the situation to their friends and relatives who had come to see them off on the platform and they too were very interested and formed a crowd round Nilima.

'Come on,' Nilima said to Raj. 'Come down.'

He looked at the station clock and saw that it was already ten minutes past the official starting time. A man in a cap blew a whistle and waved a green flag.

'Where will you go all by yourself?' Nilima said. 'What will you do?'

'They are brother and sister,' the people on the platform

said, but those in the carriage shouted down to them, 'He has taken her away from her husband's house!' A muffled voice spoke through a muffled loudspeaker, doors were slammed and porters shouted.

'You can come to see me every day!' Nilima cried through the noise. 'We will play cards and listen to the radio! It will be just like before!'

Raj found he was still holding her film-magazines. He looked at them and then at her, and he threw them to her without a word. She bent down to pick them up. The onlookers said, 'She is so young and already she has run away from her husband.' Others said, 'They learn such things from films,' and then: 'It was different in our time.'

The train started. Nilima shouted in a tearful voice, 'It will be just like before!' and she even ran for a few steps after the moving train. People shouted last greetings and instructions to each other – but they were inaudible, for the train was picking up speed and making a loud noise.

The passengers left the doors and windows. They were discussing abductions and elopements they had heard of or read about in the newspapers. It was agreed that nowadays morals were very low. Several people had interesting stories to tell in illustration of this point, and they were listened to with respect. Even those who had quarrelled about their places before were now friends and offered each other food out of their cloth bundles.

Raj took no part in any of these conversations. He remained standing by the door and held on to the rail. He wondered whether Nilima would take back the radio and the lamp and the other gifts, and he pictured to himself how disappointed Munna and Mrs. Shankar would be to lose them again so soon. A strong wind of speed rushed in through the open door and blew through his hair and his whole body; so that for the moment it was easy for him to pretend he was only a paper, a rag, a straw blown by the wind, and nothing more.

LEKHA

THE head of our department – my husband's department, that is – in the Ministry of Valuation was a widower for a long time, but when he came back from his holidays three years ago, he was married. We were all very much surprised. We had thought he was happy living alone in his government hostel; he had such a nice room there, and a good bearer, whom I myself had selected for him, and of course all we wives did our best to make him comfortable, often sending special dishes to him and arranging little dinner-parties. We were a happy group – he and the other senior officers of the department and their wives – and there was a close feeling of friendship among us all. Of course, we did have a bit of friction sometimes; for instance, I often found myself cross with Mrs. Nayyar, because I felt she was pushing herself forward too much in order to get into the Head's favour. She invited him far too often to her house, and that time he had jaundice, she went round at least twice a day to visit him. I don't like to see a lady being so forward. Anyway, it did not do her much good, because it was always obvious that the Head liked me best among all the wives. I am not boasting, I am only saying what was true and what everybody knew. I was glad that he favoured me and appreciated all the little things I was able to do for him: but I was glad not because he is the head of department and my husband's superior officer – I am not that sort of person, doing things only for my own interest, though I am afraid Mrs. Nayyar may be rather inclined that way –

but only because I have always genuinely liked him and esteemed him for his good qualities.

When we heard that he was married, we realized that things would be different now, but we hoped that our friendly relations with him would continue. Naturally, we were very eager to meet his new wife. At last the invitation came – it was for dinner – and I must admit I was rather nervous. So much depended on this lady and whether she would like me. It can be very awkward if the wife of your husband's superior officer does not like you. I know, because my sister has had a lot of trouble with the wife of her husband's Head; my sister is sure that her husband's promotion, which was due last April, did not come through only because the wife of the Head has taken a dislike to her.

In the car, on our way to the dinner, my husband said to me, 'I wonder what she is like.' He gave me a look out of the corner of his eye and said with a smile, 'I see you have made yourself very elegant to meet her.'

That annoyed me a little, so I told him, 'I don't know what you mean. Certainly I always like to look my best when people invite me out to dinner.' He did not say anything to that, so after a while I continued, 'You needn't think that I am going to put myself out very much for her. If she likes me, very well, I shall be happy. But if she is going to expect me to go down on my hands and knees to her, I'm sorry – I'm afraid I have too much pride for that.'

But as soon as I saw Lekha, I knew at once that it was going to be all right. She was young – about twenty – but not very pretty; only her eyes were nice, very large eyes which seemed to take up all her face. She was terribly nervous, and when I realized this, I at once stopped being nervous myself. I said to her, 'We have all been so eager to meet you,' in a kind and confident way. She giggled – her voice trembled so at the same time that it was almost as if she were crying – and said, 'Oh thank you, thank you!' She bit her lip, and a last strangled giggle came out, and then she was very serious.

Mrs. Nayyar, who was already sitting there on the settee with a glass of pineapple juice in her hand, cried out to me, 'Just think, she used to go to school in Bombay with my cousin!'

'Oh?' I said and sat down at some distance away from Mrs. Nayyar.

'They were in the same class. Isn't it a coincidence?' She sounded so triumphant. 'We have already found a lot to talk about.'

Lekha did not say anything for a moment, but then suddenly she started giggling again, in the same sobbing way she had done before, and she said, 'Yes, isn't it? Isn't it a coincidence?' But she seemed to be thinking of something quite different while she was saying it. Her eyes kept straying round the room, and she looked lost and unhappy about something.

I have had enough experience to recognize that look in her eyes: I knew at once that there was something wrong with the dinner. Poor little thing, I thought. And I did not like to see Mrs. Nayyar already so possessive about her: Mrs. Nayyar is quite a nice lady, but she does get very possessive about people and then she bosses them about. For instance, there is Mrs. Kaul, the wife of another senior officer, who has somehow got quite under her thumb so that she dare not say 'yes' and 'no' without first looking at Mrs. Nayyar. I didn't care for that to happen to Lekha. She seemed such an inexperienced girl; already I felt quite protective towards her.

So when she went out, I followed her and I said, 'May I

help you, please?' She answered me with the same giggle as before, saying, 'Thank you, oh no thank you, please sit comfortably.' But then she glanced up into my face – I was looking at her with a calm and kindly expression – and suddenly she threw her head against my shoulder and began to cry. I soothed her by gently patting her back.

'Oh, I don't know what to do!' she cried, wiping her eyes. 'Nothing is ready for the dinner, and it looks so terrible! How will anybody ever *eat* it?' Without another word, I walked into the kitchen. I could see at once what sort of a cook she had got. But I soon showed him that I was not a person to stand for any nonsense, so he bestirred himself as best he could and, under my directions, the dinner was somehow got ready. It was not a good dinner (it was too late for me to do anything about that) but at least we got it served, and everybody could sit down to eat.

So that was how, right from the beginning, I became Lekha's best friend. The very next day she came to see me; she sat in my drawing-room, drinking coffee and eating very many of my home-made biscuits, and talked and talked. The things she said – I had never heard anyone talk like that before. She told me all about herself and her father and the house she came from, and she told me that she loved Indian classical music and dancing and to go walking late, late at night on the beach at Bombay, and how sometimes she was very happy and sometimes so unhappy that she did not want to live any more. 'I have always been like that, since I was a child,' she told me.

'But you still are a child,' I said, smiling.

'Oh, no,' she said, 'you don't know how very serious I am inside me'; and she sighed and ate another biscuit. Of course she was very sweet, but I could not help feeling that she was hardly suitable to be the Head's wife.

She told me about her husband too : she said, 'When he came I liked him at once because he is so serious.'

'He is a very fine administrative officer,' I told her.

'Yes,' she said, rather slowly; and then, more cheerfully, though it seemed to be an effort, 'Yes, I am sure he must be.' They had been married then about five months.

After that Lekha and I used to meet several times a week. I was the only person she ever came to see; I don't think she knew anyone else in Delhi. She never cared to visit the wives of the other officers, though I know Mrs. Nayyar tried very hard to become friendly with her. But Lekha had taken a dislike to her right from the beginning. 'She is like her cousin,' she explained to me.

'Why, what is wrong with her cousin?' I asked. I was quite interested.

Lekha turned away and said, 'Please don't let us talk about her,' and her lips went tight.

'Why?' I asked. 'What has she done to you?'

'It is nothing she has done to me. It's only what she is.' Suddenly she turned to face me, and her big eyes were flashing. 'I *hate* that sort of person!' she cried. 'A person with a cold heart.' I could see that she was really filled with hate. It quite frightened me : it was so unreasonable when, as she herself admitted, the girl had done nothing to her. One did not hate people in such a way only because one disapproved of their nature. I myself disapprove of Mrs. Nayyar's nature but – God forbid – I certainly do not hate her. It is wicked to hate people.

But the next moment Lekha's face was its usual sweet childish self again. She came close to me and rubbed her cheek against mine : 'I told you we shouldn't talk about her,' she said. 'What have you and I to do with such people? You have such a dear warm nature,' she told me, and she took my hand and kissed it. She always had these soft and loving ways. 'I am so happy you are my friend,' she said.

It worried me the way Lekha did not care about her house. Mrs. Nayyar and I and all the other ladies take great pride in making our homes dainty and nice to look at. We hang up ruffled curtains and paint our own flower-vases and embroider cushions and table-runners. I am known to have quite a knack for this kind of interior decoration; everybody who comes to my house says so. Of course I wanted to help Lekha to make her home nice too. At first she was quite enthusiastic, and we went out to buy material for curtains, but then she lost interest and never even bothered to have it made up. In the end I brought my own tailor and had the curtains stitched and hung them up with my own hands. Lekha was very grateful to me and she kept saying how nice they looked; but when they became dirty, she didn't take them down to have them washed and they hung there, limp and full of dust, and in one place the curtain-ring was torn off and not sewn back again.

The trouble with Lekha was that she was not modern. She simply did not understand the new trends we have in India today. Of course we are all very proud of being Indian, but all the same we do realize that there are some things we can learn from the West. The Western way of doing up a house and living in it, for example, is more attractive and advanced than ours. Lekha kept far too much to the old Indian ways. When she was alone, she never sat down to eat properly at a table but squatted on the floor and had her food brought to her on a round brass tray, and then ate it with her fingers. That may be the traditional Indian way, but it is my opinion that it is not a nice way and that it would be better for India if everyone learned to eat in the way people do in the West. Anyway, what is the sense in using these old-fashioned brass trays and bowls when you can get such pretty china nowadays? I also didn't like the way Lekha had incense burning in her house; that smell always reminds me of the dirty little shops in the bazaar.

It was not as if she were at all orthodox – I have never known her to go to the temple – and yet she kept so many of the old customs, which advanced people have long ago abandoned. When it was some fast-day she would fast, from sunset to sunset; on the day of the Spring Festival she would wear only yellow, just like the peasants do; once, when there was an eclipse, she even went down to the Jumna to bathe there, with all the crowd. Some of our old customs are very pretty, I know – the lighting of little lamps on Diwali, for instance, which we always do because the children like it so much – but it is not in keeping with modern times to observe as many of them as Lekha did. And as if there were not enough Hindu festivals, she would keep the Muslim ones also, such as Mohurrum and Bakri-Id-ul-Fitr, when she had some goat-meat cooked and sent to our house. When I asked her about this, she said, 'Oh you know, I love festivals so much, it doesn't matter whether they are Hindu or Muslim. And anyway, I think there is bound to be some Muslim strain in all of us, so it is only right that we should keep their holy days.' I am all for Hindu–Muslim unity myself, but I think that is carrying it too far. The only festival she would not keep was Christmas. I think Christmas is such a nice festival; we always have a turkey dinner with plum pudding, and so do all our friends. But Lekha said she did not like Christmas, because it is not religious. She said it is only social and only for Englishmen. When I pointed out to her that, on the contrary, Christmas is very religious because it is the day on which the God of the Christians was born, she said that yes, she liked Jesus

Christ, but she did not like Christians or their Christmas. What can you say to a person like that?

It surprised me that the Head allowed her to carry on with all these fads. He himself has always been very correct in his behaviour, and one would have thought that he was the last person to allow his wife to go in for practices that were so unsuitable to their high social and official position. But apparently he made no objections and let her do whatever she pleased. I think he had grown very fond of Lekha. It is not easy to tell the feelings of a man like him. Although he is always very kind and considerate, there is nevertheless something very serious and correct about him which keeps people at a distance. The expression on his face is rather severe, and this rarely alters, whatever his feelings might be. And yet I thought I could detect a change in him, that something had come into his face that had not been there before; something that showed he was – I don't know quite how to say it – perhaps 'satisfied' is what I mean; or perhaps happy.

Lekha never enjoyed the little dinner-parties we gave. She came once or twice to dinners at Mrs. Nayyar's house or Mrs. Kaul's or one of the other wives', but it was quite evident that she did not enjoy herself. She made hardly any attempts to join in the conversation – the gentlemen usually discuss office affairs and we ladies talk about our children and servants and the house and other things of interest to us – but she would just sit there quite quiet with her head bowed and playing with her bangles. Then, one day when Mrs. Nayyar was giving a dinner-party, the Head telephoned in the afternoon to say his wife was ill and so unfortunately they could not come. I went to see Lekha straightaway next morning, but when I asked her what was the matter, she laughed out loud. 'Only Mrs. Nayyar's party was the matter!' she said. 'No, I have had enough now of these little dinner-parties. I have done my duty.'

'Lekha,' I said, quite shocked, for I myself was giving a party the following week, 'are you telling me that you are not coming to *any* of our parties again?'

'I will come to your house,' she said, 'but to nobody else. Why should I sit there and die with boredom while everyone talks stupid things? I will sit at home and think my own stupid things.'

I always feel rather nervous before my dinner-parties, so you can imagine that I was not at all pleased when Govind suddenly appeared at my house half an hour before the guests were due to arrive. Govind is my husband's younger brother, but he is as unlike my husband as can be. He finished his studies at the university, but after that he never made any attempts to get into government service or into any proper job at all. He only sits in coffee-houses all day, with other loafers like himself; sometimes he does something for films or radio – I don't know what. He associates a great deal with musicians and dancers and such-like people, and I'm afraid that there are some not very nice rumours regarding his behaviour with women.

I did not even pretend to be pleased to see him. I said, 'I didn't know you were in Delhi.' He spends most of his time in Bombay where I think there are even more loafers for him to sit with than here.

'I have been here for three weeks,' he said and laughed; he laughs a great deal.

'And only now you have come to see your elder brother.'

'But you are never happy to see me,' he said. That was true, but I didn't think it was right for him to say it. Just then my husband came in, and the two of them greeted one another. My husband is quite fond of his brother, though of course he disapproves strongly of his ways. 'Where are you staying?' he asked him and Govind said, 'Here, there and everywhere.' He always stays with his useless friends when he comes to Delhi; about four of them crowd together into some little room in one of those cheap boarding-houses which are always smelling of coffee and South Indian food.

While the two brothers talked, I thought desperately about how to fit Govind into my dinner-party. He was quite unsuitable to meet the Head and all the other officers, who are all serious and important government servants. Even his clothes were unsuitable; the others would all be coming in evening-dress, but he was wearing his usual wide white pyjama trousers with a loose and very thin Lucknow kurta on top. He keeps his hair, which is deep black and curly, rather too long, and this gives him a not quite respectable appearance.

But it turned out that I need not have worried after all. Govind knows how to behave when he wants to, and that evening he really acquitted himself very well. He took an interest in the office affairs the gentlemen were discussing and asked some quite intelligent questions, which the Head answered for him in a clear precise way; and he was very attentive and polite to the ladies. Indeed, I could see at once that Mrs. Nayyar felt flattered by the way he got fruit-juice and nuts for her and found her handbag when she mislaid it. A little later, after the buffet dinner (when there are more than six people we always have buffet because our dining-table does not seat more than six) I noticed Govind talking to Lekha. He was sitting on the arm of her chair, holding his plate and swinging one foot, and she was looking up at him. If Lekha had not happened to be the Head's wife, I must say I would have felt embarrassed for her appearance. She was wearing an orange cotton sari – *cotton!* for a dinner-party! – and, as usual, no lipstick. She had the tikka mark on her forehead, and she had stained the palms of her hands and the soles of her feet with henna to make them bright orange, which I think is such a dirty habit, even though it may be an old tradition. There she was, looking up at Govind with her big big eyes which appeared even bigger because she had underlined them with black kohl; the two of them seemed to have a lot to talk about. I must say, they fitted well together, both of them so odd in their appearance and so different from the rest of us. They looked like a couple out of Hindu mythology – the sort of Krishna and Radha couple you see on calendars or in historical films.

The day after my party, Sita, my eldest child, got measles, and after that my son got it too, and finally the baby. It was a very hectic time for me, and it was three weeks before I could leave the house again. The very first day I went out, though I had many errands to do, I made a point of going to Lekha's house. I still felt responsible for her, and I knew I was her only friend. The servant showed me straight into the drawing-room, where I found Lekha sitting on the floor. Lying beside her, with his head in her lap, was Govind. She was stroking his hair. They started up when they saw me, and Lekha came flying to meet me. She embraced me with great fervour and said, 'I am so happy to see you, so happy!' Really, I have never known anyone sound so happy.

I sat down and I said, 'How are you, Lekha?' I felt terribly shaken with shock, and my heart had become heavy and cold inside me. Govind lay down on the floor again and he supported his head on his hand. I didn't want to look at him, but I could not help myself, and I saw he was smiling. Lekha was also smiling, and laughing, and she kept talking all the time. I could not take in one half of all she was saying, I was so upset and she was talking so fast. She asked after Sita and the other two children and my husband and what we had been doing, a hundred things she was asking but she never waited for a reply, and all the time she didn't really seem to be asking those questions, but something else, her voice was full of something else. Govind did not say anything, but sometimes he would laugh at something she said, and then she would cry, 'No, you mustn't laugh at me! Tell him not to laugh at me!' But she laughed too. I told her I had to go, I had an appointment with the dentist – I made up a lie on the spur of the moment – and I went out without saying anything at all to Govind. Lekha saw me to the door, and there she embraced me again. 'I'll come and see you tomorrow,' she said. 'I have so much to tell you!' Suddenly she kissed me on the neck; her lips and breath were very hot.

When I got home, I lay down on the bed and shut my eyes. But I could not get rid of the picture of the two of them together as I had seen them when I came in, or the sound of the laughter between them. It was such a great shock to me, and not only because it was Lekha and Govind – though that in itself was bad enough and would get worse when I grew calm enough to think about it. But to see two people behaving like that, a man and a woman together! Oh, it was nothing really that they did; it was only the understanding between them, and something else that I can't describe – something that had come rising out of them and filled the room. Sitting there with them had been like sitting together with two naked people. It made me feel so much ashamed. I have been married now for ten years and I am fond of my husband and I have had three children by him, but we have always used restraint in our behaviour together. I pressed my face into my pillow and suddenly I began to cry. I don't know why I cried, but I cried very bitterly.

By the time Lekha came to see me the next morning, I was quite calm and collected. I had not told my husband anything of what I had discovered. I didn't want to worry him – he has enough worries in his office – and also I felt shy to tell him. I did not know how to put it into words for him. So I determined to deal with this thing myself. I would talk to Lekha; I would be very strict with her. I would make her see her sin and folly, and then she would not meet Govind any more.

But when she came, it was she who did all the talking. She came running into the house with her arms full of toys for the children: 'How are they?' she cried. 'How is my Sita?' And when they came, she embraced them and kissed them – something she had never done before – and they were very pleased with the toys. Then she turned to me and her eyes were shining and her bosom heaving up and down and she said, 'Oh, I love you all so!' There was a great change in her: she had become beautiful. Her movements had always been a little awkward, but now they were light and graceful. She tossed back her hair, stretched out her arms, walked up and down – she couldn't sit still for a minute – and her bangles jingled, her eyes were brilliant and she was laughing, laughing all the time.

'I am so happy!' she said to me. 'You don't know how happy!' Here I should have started telling her what I had meant to tell her, but she would not give me time. 'I didn't know there was anyone so wonderful as he in the world!'

she said. I wanted to protest – I had known Govind a good deal longer than she, and there was no one who knew his worth (or, rather, lack of it) better than I – but she went on again immediately. 'There is such depth in him, such greatness! Oh I know, he hasn't done anything great yet, but he will. Only wait and you'll see! He will astonish the world!'

If the situation had not been so serious, I could have burst out laughing at the idea of Govind astonishing the world. If sitting idly in coffee-houses will astonish the world, then certainly he will do it, but not otherwise.

'I feel so privileged to be allowed to know him,' she said; and in a whisper, 'And to be loved by him.'

'Lekha,' I said.

'You don't know what happiness he gives me, what a paradise he has made for me.'

'Lekha,' I said, 'are you in your senses?'

'Oh no, no! I have taken leave of my senses! I have no mind any more – only a body and a soul! He has awakened both for me. You don't know, you don't know what it is like to be loved by such a man. . . .'

I said, quietly and sternly, 'And your husband?'

'Please don't!' she cried and put up her hands to cover her ears. 'Why do you talk of him? What has he to do with this?'

I was aghast at such total irresponsibility, but I managed to say quite calmly: 'I should have thought your husband had a great deal to do with it.'

'Nothing! Believe me, this is different – Oh believe me . . .' She stood still and put both her arms up to her head to stroke back her hair and her eyes shone more brightly than ever. I felt embarrassed to look at her.

'He is good and kind, I know —' she said and I took her

up, rather severely, 'The Head is an excellent man in every way.'

'I know, I know!' she cried. 'But being good and kind is so little – it is nothing, by being only good and kind you can't touch another person's soul. I was not alive before,' she said and turned to look at me with her big burning eyes. 'Nobody could show me what there was in me till he came.' And she added, in a small humble voice, 'I feel so grateful to him.'

Then I only wanted that she should go away. I kept remembering the way her lips and breath had been so hot, when she had kissed me. But she wouldn't go: she kept talking, on and on, about herself and Govind. I sat quite still and tried not to listen, but I couldn't help listening. There was something burning and fierce about her, like fire.

After that she often came to see me and every time it was the same. She talked, and I had to sit and listen to things that should never be spoken. She had no shame at all. She talked to me about the beauty of Govind and how she too had learnt to feel her body as beautiful. It was terrible for me to have to hear such things: and worse, the tone of her voice, her gestures, the way she moved, everything about her expressed exactly what she was saying, so that even without her words one could sense the sinful passion into which she had flung herself. It was painful for me even to look at her and, after some time, I began to avoid her. I would go out of the house at the times I knew she would be coming to visit me. I did not care where I went, so long as I didn't have to see her and listen to her. Mostly I went to Mrs. Nayyar, where we would sit and talk quietly and normally about normal things, like the children's schooling and the high price of vegetables and the lovely new Benaras saris which had come in at the Cottage In-

dustries Emporium. These conversations with Mrs. Nayyar were soothing to me; yet all the same when I got home
it was not of her I thought but of Lekha and Govind. I
became very irritable, especially with my husband; somehow I had a feeling of dissatisfaction about him.

Some time later it was my turn again to give a dinner-
party, and of course I had to invite the Head and Lekha.
When the guests were all assembled, Govind walked in. I
knew only too well who had told him to come, but with all
those people there I had to pretend to be pleased to see
him and make him welcome. He was as usual very free and
smiling in his behaviour, and not in the least embarrassed.
It was I who was embarrassed. Lekha had told me so often,
'He is like a god, handsome like a god,' and I had always
wondered how she could be so blind. But now I saw that
there was something about him that might perhaps strike
an impressionable person like Lekha, though speaking for
myself I have an aversion against that type of looks. His
complexion is rather too dark – my husband, thank God, is
much fairer – and against this dark skin his teeth, which are
very strong and healthy, and the whites of his eyes shine quite
brilliantly. He has strong shoulders, and because he always
wears such thin transparent kurtas one can see exactly how
they are formed and how the muscles move. His hair is
really far too long and it is very curly and shines with oil.
He always wears a fine gold chain round his neck. His voice
and also his movements are very soft.

I watched the two of them anxiously, but I must say their
behaviour was quite good. I never intercepted as much as a
glance between them, and they talked together very little.
Govind circulated freely among the other guests; he de-
voted a lot of attention to Mrs. Nayyar, who was quite
delighted by him. Lekha was more lively than she usually

is at parties, for which I suppose I ought to have been grateful. The Head seemed pleased to see her enjoying herself, and I noticed that he still looked at her with an expression of satisfaction.

The talk turned to a celebrated South Indian dancer who had given a recital in Delhi the week before; and from there a discussion arose about the various styles of dancing and their exponents. We always like to keep in touch with these cultural matters. I must say, Govind talked quite intelligently and managed to impress the other guests with his knowledge of Indian classical music and dancing: he had always taken a great interest in these things – far too great an interest, for it is hardly proper for a man to devote as much time and attention to them as he does. Mrs. Nayyar, I could see, was thrilled by all he was telling us, and the Head too listened with interest. Then suddenly the Head said, 'You know, my wife is quite a competent exponent of Bharata Natyam,' and he smiled in a deprecating but rather proud manner.

'Oh yes? How interesting,' said Govind, and he looked around as if he were not quite sure who the Head's wife was; really, he should have been an actor.

Mrs. Nayyar clapped her hands together and cried, 'Oh, but why doesn't she dance for us?' She always likes to be lively at parties, and now of course she was being specially lively for Govind's benefit. Mrs. Kaul, who has got into the habit of doing exactly what Mrs. Nayyar does, also exclaimed, 'Wouldn't that be lovely!' So then everybody looked at Lekha who laughed and said, 'Should I?' She was not at all shy or embarrassed.

Govind said, 'It would be a great pleasure for all of us.'

'Yes, wouldn't it,' I said quickly, 'but there are no ankle-bells and no music, what a pity.'

'She could perhaps have Sita's ankle-bells?' Govind suggested. 'And you have a dholak, I think?'

'What are we waiting for?' cried Mrs. Nayyar.

I looked at the Head; I was sure he would not allow it. But he smiled and, passing his hand down his cheeks and chin, said, 'Well, Government is always telling us that we must preserve and foster our cultural heritage . . .'

I hoped that Sita's ankle-bells would be too small for Lekha, but they weren't. Her limbs were as thin and fragile as a child's. Govind sat on the floor by the dholak and began to beat it with his fingers and sing, while Lekha danced. He sang:

'Bring, O bring, my beloved unto me!
O what ecstasy shall I know with him always on the
couch strewn with flowers, in the white radiance of
the moon.
O my friend, beautiful as a bird! I languish with
love for my lord.
What is this happening to me? Come, O friend!
Ask my lord to come to me, so that flower-adorned I may
dance, sing and play with him. Why this delay?'

And that was what Lekha danced. She really was quite a good dancer. Her hand gestures were very suggestive, and so was her smile, and the way she rolled her eyes and swayed her head from her neck. 'I languish with love for my lord,' said her fingers. 'What is this happening to me?' said her eyes and her lips. The ankle-bells rang out as she stamped her feet. 'O what ecstasy shall I know with him always!' Govind flung back his head so that one could see the movement in his throat as he sang; his long brown fingers danced on the drum, his whole body swayed; he was smiling all the time so that his teeth and eyes flashed. 'Like a god,' she had said, 'he is handsome like a god'; and now she was worshipping him with her dance – how soft she looked, how pleading – and he knew it and she knew it and I knew it. Mrs. Nayyar sat with her head to one side and a smile of rapture on her face. The Head was also smiling, and he beat time in the air with one hand, and looked so proud. As I glanced at him, I thought how good he is – how true, how affectionate, and how stupid!

A week later Govind went away to Bombay – I think on some film work. When he had gone, Lekha came to see me every day. If I was out, as I often tried to be, she would sit and wait for me, and the moment I came in she would begin to talk about herself and Govind. His absence did not seem to make her at all sad. 'You see, he has not gone away from me,' she told me. 'He is with me here' – and she clasped her hand to her bosom in such a passionate gesture that I had to look down to study my toe-nails. 'All the time,' she said, and shut her eyes, 'all the time.' Another day she told me, 'You remember how when Krishna went away from Radha? How she thought she could hear his flute playing, even when he was not there? It is like that with me. I can feel him playing in my heart.' She had told him to send letters to her at my house. 'Because I know you are my friend,' she said to me and she took my hand and kissed it; so I could not say anything. But there were no letters. Every day she came with such a trembling air of expectation, but every day there was nothing. I could see the disappointment in her face, though she always tried to disguise it. 'There is no need for him to write,' she explained. 'He knows how near we are together, even when we are apart.' I think she wrote to him every day.

After some time she didn't come to see me so often, and when she came she didn't talk much any more. She sat quietly in my drawing-room, playing with the bangles on her arms. She was thin and her lips were pale, and it was hard for me to imagine how I had ever come to think of her as beautiful. Now it was I who did most of the talking, but she never seemed to take any interest in what I was telling her. Conversation with Mrs. Nayyar was really far more stimulating. I couldn't help thinking that Lekha was rather a dull girl, but all the same I began to feel protective towards her again, and to like her as I had in the beginning.

Then a whole week went by with no visit from her, and I became worried and went to see her one morning. She was sitting in her drawing-room, on the floor, with her knees drawn up and her arms clasped round them. Although it was after eleven o'clock, she had not yet had her bath or dressed, and her hair straggled over her shoulders in a very untidy manner. The room smelled of stale incense, and I could see at once that it had not been dusted or tidied for many days.

She did not move when I came in; she hardly even smiled. 'Hallo, Lekha!' I called in a cheerful voice. I felt so fresh and vigorous after my morning bath, in my crisp clean sari and with my household duties all ordered and done.

But all she gave me in response was a sad look, and she lifted one hand to brush a strand of hair from her forehead. I wanted to shake her and shout, 'Come on, Lekha! Up and doing!' I wanted to fling open all the windows and call in the servant to give the room a good scrubbing and cleaning, and then bring fresh flowers to arrange on the mantelpiece and a clean starched cloth to put on the table. But I realized that my first duty was to give Lekha a good talking-to, so I sat down on the settee just behind her, with my hand laid affectionately on her shoulder.

I didn't know how I was going to start, but the words

came of themselves – all the words I had been wanting to say for many weeks but which she had never given me any opportunity to say. First I talked to her about her husband – about what a fine, good, conscientious man he was, and what she owed to him as his wife. And after that I told her what a worthless loafer Govind was, who never did any work and associated with people who were not respectable; I even gave her a hint of rumours I had heard of his behaviour with a certain type of woman in Bombay. I talked for a long time. She sat quite still, with her head bowed, and the only movement she made was once when she shrugged the shoulder on which I had laid my hand. I thought it might be making her feel hot – it was rather sticky that morning – so I took it away. She did not see me to the door when I left, but remained sitting there on the floor. I felt pleased and contented all the rest of the day, for I knew I had done my duty; in the evening I made my husband take me to a cinema.

I telephoned to her the next day, but the servant said she was out; the day after that it was the same, and the day after. I was rather surprised, for I knew she never went out anywhere unless it was to come and see me. So on the fourth day I went to her house. When I entered at the gate, I saw her sitting on the veranda, but she got up at once and went indoors. I thought she had not seen me, and I was about to follow her, when the servant came running out, waving his arms at me and shouting, 'Memsahib has gone out!'

I realized then that Lekha did not wish to see me any more. I went home and sat in my bedroom and cried. But I didn't cry long, for I knew that I had acted rightly in every way, and that if Lekha had been a person of principle, she would have understood that and felt grateful towards me. I had nothing to reproach myself with. If Lekha cared to take up such an attitude, I could not help it. At any rate, I had done my duty.

One morning, not so long ago, I finished my shopping a little earlier than usual, so there was just time to drop in at Mrs. Nayyar's for a chat and perhaps a cup of coffee (though the coffee she serves is never very good). I came by the veranda, and I was just going to enter the drawing-room through the open glass doors when I heard a voice say, 'I don't know how it is, sometimes I'm so happy, so happy – and sometimes I'm so sad that I don't want to live any more.' I stood quite still and then I looked through the door, and, yes, there was Lekha, curled up on a rug in Mrs. Nayyar's drawing-room, talking with great animation and nibbling home-made biscuits. I wanted to go away, but unfortunately Mrs. Nayyar caught sight of me and called out, 'Hallo, there! What a surprise!'

Lekha got up at once and said, 'I must go.' She had averted her head from me and was playing with her bangles.

'So soon?' said Mrs. Nayyar, and she put her arm round Lekha's shoulders to walk with her to the door. I heard them whispering together outside, and then I think they kissed each other good-bye.

'Poor Lekha,' said Mrs. Nayyar, coming back into the drawing-room wearing her big, pleased smile. 'She is such a shy little thing. Whenever anybody comes, she rushes off at once. A cup of coffee?' She poured the coffee and then sat on the settee, stirring the sugar in her cup. 'Yes,' she said, 'Lekha is very shy before others. But when we are alone together, she sits and talks and talks for hours. She tells me everything. Everything,' she said again, stirring, and looking as if she had a big secret. I also stirred. After a while she leaned close to me and continued in a low voice, 'You know, she has had a great love affair with an artist.' I kept looking down into my coffee cup. 'They were terribly in love,' Mrs. Nayyar went on, and her eyes shone. 'But then Lekha sent him away. Because of the Head. She says she couldn't do anything to hurt the Head. How fine,' she said in a voice full of feeling. 'How noble.' I sipped the coffee, which was, as I had expected, of a rather inferior quality.

The only times I ever see Lekha nowadays are at one of Mrs. Nayyar's dinner-parties. She won't come to any of our other parties, and at Mrs. Nayyar's she only sits there and plays with her bangles. She never as much as looks at me. Mrs. Nayyar has told me in confidence that Lekha has told her she does not like me because I am a person with a cold heart. I think that is a very unfair and unkind thing to say about me, especially after I have been such a good friend to her. But what distresses me most is that because of Lekha's attitude towards me we can no longer have any social relations with the Head. I know it will not make any difference in the end, because he is really too fair-minded a person to let personal considerations stand in the way of his official reports. But I am sorry to have lost contact with him, because I have always had a genuine liking and respect for him. He is such a good man. Often I can't help thinking that it is a pity he could not have married a wife who would do more credit to his office. After all, being the wife of the head of a department carries a lot of responsibilities. If my husband – please God – ever attains to such a high position, I certainly shall not shirk them the way Lekha has done.

SIXTH CHILD

THE pains started early in the morning and at once the house was full of busy women. It was amazing how quickly they came, some of them from right across the other side of the town. Babu Ram never could understand how women managed to get news so quickly; a deathbed, a lying-in, sickness, accident, any sudden blow of fortune or misfortune, and all the female relations were there without delay. The men always tended to fall into the background on these occasions; especially of course at a lying-in. Never did Babu Ram feel so awkward, useless, unwanted and embarrassed as he did in his own house every time his wife had a new baby.

He wandered around aimlessly, with sad eyes and an apologetic smile, trying to keep out of the way of the women, who rushed around full of purpose and determination. He would have liked to talk to his little girls, but a squad of women had taken charge of them and were washing, brushing, scrubbing, feeding and dressing them prior to pushing them off to someone else's house, where they were to stay till it was all over and the baby safely born. Babu Ram felt as sorry for his little girls as he did for himself. The five of them looked so subdued, with their faces scrubbed terribly clean, their hair oiled and pulled tight from their foreheads. They kept quite still, their eyes huge with wonder: whereas usually they were as quick and twittering as birds. Babu Ram wanted to throw them some word of encouragement but was himself feeling too subdued and discouraged to be able to do so. All he could manage was a very shy smile as they were bundled out of the house; they looked back at him with big, silent eyes.

At last one of the women deigned to notice him – his mother's cousin, a short, square old woman who was always very prominent on these occasions, walking around with her elbows stuck out and a pleased, busy look on her face. 'Now then,' she said to him, 'what are you still doing here? Be off with you!' 'Yes,' he said, passing his hand over his balding head, 'yes, it is time I went to the shop.' Another woman called out, 'Don't let us see your face again too quickly! Your work is done – now it is our turn!' He simpered and shifted uneasily from one leg to the other. 'Come back tonight and see what we have for you,' said his mother's cousin and brushed past him into the room where his wife lay groaning on a string-bed.

He put on his little round hat and walked slowly down the stairs. Plump and neat, with his dhoti falling in tidy folds around his legs and exposing his fat, smooth calves above his highly polished black shoes, he looked as comfortable as he did every morning when he left thus, clean and breakfasted, for the shop. But he did not feel comfortable at all. He was worrying about his little girls and about himself, both driven out of the house so unceremoniously; and also about something else, which he did not dare think about much. But downstairs he met the first-floor tenant who said to him, 'So it has started,' and then, 'well, let us hope this time. . . .'

'Yes,' said Babu Ram, lifting his hat from his head with both hands and then settling it back again. 'Yes,' he said, and couldn't say anything further, because he hoped so much that he trembled when he thought about it. He stood on the bottom step, with his head lowered and looking, in spite of his comfortable confident paunch, almost humble.

'God will be good to you,' his neighbour – himself the father of four sons – comforted him. 'He knows five daughters is enough for anyone.' And he laughed with the easy heartiness of a man to whom the topic doesn't matter much. Babu Ram also tried to laugh, but as it mattered a great deal to him, could not do so at all heartily.

His younger brother, Siri Ram, had already opened the shop, as he did every morning, and sat inside eating his breakfast from a leaf which he held in the hollow of his hand. Babu Ram stepped out of his shoes and into the shop. He hung up his hat on the appointed nail and sat down on the white sheet spread on the floor, with his legs tucked underneath him. Quickly his eyes ranged to the right, to the left, and behind him, over the shelves piled with bolts of cloth, row upon row, up to the roof of his little hut of a shop. Tomorrow he would have to take down the pink and green muslin from Kanpur, which had not sold at all well and was getting faded, to make room for a consignment of flowered white lawn he was expecting from Bombay.

Siri Ram licked his fingers, all ten one after the other, and said, 'How is it going?' Babu Ram replied by shrugging one shoulder and looking resigned.

'It always takes time,' said Siri Ram, speaking with authority, for though he was still a very young man, he already had four children of his own.

Babu Ram grunted, then said, 'See that you have all this month's sales tax-vouchers – otherwise those Government people will come sitting on my head again.' He spoke in a brisk business voice, for he did not want Siri Ram to know how much he was thinking about the baby.

It was a morning like every morning. Quiet, with not many people in the bazaar, and the shopkeepers sitting crosslegged in their shops, some smoking their hookahs and some saying their prayers and some writing business letters and some doing the 'Win 10,000 Rupees' crossword puzzle. Tall glasses of buttermilk, frothing with cream, arrived from Lal Singh's Milkshop of Lahore and hot fritters with chutney from the Peshawar Famous Hotel. There was a little desultory conversation across the narrow lanes which ran between the rows of shops, and a few hawkers walked about calling digestive powders or elastic, though not very lustily because there weren't many customers about. Babu Ram did accounts, he sat on the floor with his big ledger in front of him and his spectacles perched on the end of his nose, and he stroked his hand up and down his paunch which flowed gently over his thighs. Now and again a customer came, and Siri Ram brought down bolt after bolt of cloth until the floor of the shop was covered in a flood of shining new materials; after the customer had gone, Siri Ram patiently rolled them all up again.

Though he tried to concentrate on his accounts, Babu Ram could not help thinking more of the son he was hoping for so much. It was the sixth time he was hoping for one and he was afraid of being disappointed for the sixth time. Not that he did not love his five little daughters. His heart turned over every time he thought of them – quick, skinny, demure in their wide trousers with the flowered shirts over them, their hair tight in thin pigtails, their huge eyes full of wonder and shyness, their piping voices which always sounded excited. But he longed for a son. There were all the obvious reasons why he must have a son (who, otherwise, would preside over his funeral obsequies and pour the ghee to feed the cremating fire? Who would carry on the shop, the properties?). But there were also other reasons, less obvious and closer to his heart.

Perhaps what he really wanted was to have, like the other

shopkeepers, a little boy to sit with him in the shop. It was
in the evenings that he most felt the lack of such a little boy.
The bazaar became very busy in the evenings; shoppers
thronged the narrow lanes between the shops, there was a
lot of buying and selling and haggling, hawkers cried their
wares, beggars whined for alms. But inside the shops it
remained private and cosy. When one walked through the
bazaar, each shop with its open front was like a photograph
of a family group exposed to view in a big square of electric
light; one could see the shopkeeper and his assistants (who
were of course members of the family – a younger brother,
an impoverished uncle, a nephew) talking to their customers, who sat on a narrow bench and looked critically at
the goods shown to them. Here the bargaining was quieter
and interspersed now with gossip and now with philosophy;
glasses of cool water were offered; everything was calm,
leisured, very polite. And always, in almost every shop,
there was a little boy. He sat at the edge of the shop, with
his legs dangling over. Sometimes he did his homework, or
ate gram out of a paper cone. It was obvious – perhaps from
the fearless, even arrogant way he looked at the passers-by
and the customers – that he was quite at home and at ease
in the shop; that he knew himself to have every right to be
there; that it was, in fact, his father's shop.

With little girls it was different. They had to stay at home
with the women of the family, where they became as familiar
with the life of kitchen and courtyard as the boys did with
that of the shop. They learned to imitate the ways of grandmother, mother, aunts, pretended to wear saris and to
pound spices and sift rice and scold servants. How often
Babu Ram had watched them at their games, chuckling to
himself, his heart all glowing with love! Yet at the same
time there was always a trace of regret: because he felt that

there should also be a little boy to play at doing as the father did – to wear a dhoti and a little round hat and pretend to be a shopkeeper. He could almost see this little boy following him down the stairs of the house on their way to the shop, treading in his footsteps and trying to look just like him – tucking in his chin, frowning as he adjusted his hat, clearing his throat in a proud parody of his father's manner.

He had never, he thought, as he sat in his shop seemingly intent over his accounts and calmly stroking his belly, wanted anything so much. He felt tense with the anxiety of wanting. Siri Ram sat at the other side of the shop with his knees drawn up, looking out with vacant eyes and picking his nose. Babu Ram could not talk to him. Yet he wanted terribly to unburden himself to someone and have him share his weight of anxiety. Perhaps not share, though: what he really wanted was for someone to relieve him of it, someone to come and say, 'Don't worry any more – this time you will have a son.' But who could say that to him? Except perhaps God.

He believed of course in God and did all the things that he knew were required to please Him. Thus he had accompanied his wife several times on the daily visits she made to the temple during her pregnancy, had made his offerings of flowers and sweetmeats and had vowed to feast 500 Brahmins if his prayers were granted. But all the same he could not help feeling that there was something more he should do. Prayers and offerings were too remote and impersonal; they were what one did, as a duty, on all occasions. Now he wanted to please God with something more direct, more spontaneous, more personal – something exceptional to prove himself worthy of the great favour he was asking.

Tumblers of buttermilk arrived from Lal Singh's Milkshop. Siri Ram made loud noises of relish from behind his

tumbler. 'Ah!' said Siri Ram, 'Hah!' But Babu Ram hardly noticed himself drinking; he was thinking how unworthy he was and how presumptuous it was in him to expect God to favour him. He felt that in his present sinful state he did not deserve a son and that, to become worthy in the sight of God, he had somehow to cleanse and purify himself. To be a better man, that was what he wanted, to rid himself of his past sins and imperfections. . . .

When he thought of his past sins and imperfections, he thought really of only one incident. God knew, there were plenty more (after all, in business life one could not always think as much of others as perhaps it was right to do, and he with his many dependants had to put his family and their interests above all else); but none of them disturbed his conscience the way this one did. He could still see the old man's face with its expression of patience and resignation; and himself shouting abuses, his face swollen with rage. Oh yes, of course, he had been right to shout abuses and turn the old man out of the house. Everybody said he had been right. Everybody had abused the old man because of the way he had stolen from Babu Ram who was his cousin and who had kept him for many years and had always been so kind to him. 'Ungrateful devil!' they had shouted. 'Thief, liar, cheat!' Babu Ram shouted loudest of all; he felt rage throttling him till it was difficult for him to get the words out, and then in his fury he even slapped the old man – one! two! across the face – the way he might have slapped Siri Ram or some other younger brother over whom he had been set in authority. 'Quite right!' they all shouted. 'With shoes he should be beaten!' The old man stood quite silent and patient, as if he were waiting for Babu Ram to take off his slipper and start beating him with it. This silence infuriated Babu Ram more than ever: there was something like innocence and martyrdom in it. When of course it was quite clear that the old man *had* stolen from the shop, consistently and unscrupulously and, moreover, surprisingly large amounts. 'Get out!' Babu Ram screamed, his hands twitching so that he was almost afraid of his own anger. The old man quietly rolled up his things. Babu Ram could still see him walking away with slow steps and eyes downcast, the little bundle of his possessions under his arm.

He drank the last of his buttermilk, holding the glass with one hand, and shutting his account book with the other. He shut it with a snap to suggest to himself the finality of his resolution. He would go and get the old man back. Now, at once. He got up, adjusted his dhoti and took his hat down from its nail. Siri Ram, one finger probing inside a nostril, looked up at him in surprise. 'I am going out,' Babu Ram said sternly. 'If that man comes from Sita Mills, you can tell him to come to me tomorrow. Today I have urgent work.'

'You are going home? To see about the baby? But it will be many hours yet. . . .'

'What concern is it of yours where I am going?' Babu Ram said, frowning with terrible authority. He didn't want anyone to know. They would all know soon enough; they would be angry with him and say he was a fool. 'Perhaps we have not enough mouths to feed in this house?' his wife would reproach him. But Babu Ram wanted the old man back: to wipe out that moment when he had been angry and the old man had stood patient and silent; to make himself worthy of a son.

He knew that the old man had gone to live with another group of relatives, who were only remotely connected with Babu Ram's own particular branch of the family. He sat in a

cycle rickshaw and had himself taken straight there. The
house was behind a temple, so it was hedged in by many
little stalls selling flower garlands and sweetmeats and
plaster-of-paris images of the gods. Pilgrims sat resting by
the side of the road and there were clusters of ascetics in
orange robes on the steps of the temple and a few dirty grey
cows walking about and pariah dogs snuffling in the gutter
for refuse. Babu Ram haggled for a while with the rickshaw
driver and then went into the house, calling in a hesitant
voice, 'Is anyone here?' But the house was quite silent, sunk
in midday heat and sleep. All the men were probably out,
and the women and servants resting in cool rooms after their
meal. Babu Ram stood in the passage, scratching his head
under his little round hat and not quite knowing what to do.
He did not want to go farther for fear of intruding into the
women's quarter. Yet it was in the women's quarter that he
would be most likely to find the old man, who had always
had a predilection for sitting in that part of a house; so
much so that, in his younger days, they had called him 'the
eunuch'. But it was in the women's quarter that his two
only interests in life were centred – food and children. He
was an amazing eater, everybody knew that; and everybody
also knew that there was no one who could amuse children
the way he could. Babu Ram's five little girls had loved him,
they had clustered around him, clambered on his back, on
his knees, up his arms, piping in shrill voices, 'Uncle, tell
us a story!' 'Uncle, make us a kite!' 'Uncle, be a train with
a engine!' And the old man had laughed and tried to defend
himself, crying, 'But wait a minute, just one minute!' For
the first few weeks after he left the house, they had often
asked after him and had to be promised that he would come
back soon. Now of course they had almost forgotten him;
children were like that.

Babu Ram cleared his throat and called again, 'Is anyone here?' Suddenly from the temple, bursting into the still, hot afternoon with an air of great joyousness, came the sound of chanting accompanied by the tinkling of tiny cymbals. Now too there was a faint stirring from inside the house. Babu Ram heard a woman's voice, heavy with sleep, in some inner room, and a jingling of keys and bangles, and then the woman came shuffling out on naked feet. She was a young, fat, healthy woman, and she was rubbing her eyes which were still full of sleep; she must have washed her hair before lying down, for it hung, damp and glistening, along her back, wave upon wave down to her waist. 'Every time we sleep they wake us with their prayers,' she muttered crossly, standing in the doorway, scratching under her armpit and looking at Babu Ram with bleary eyes. The chanting continued loud and joyful. Babu Ram joined his palms together in greeting and said, 'How are you, sister.' She blinked at him a few times, leaning her heavy weight against the doorframe, and then recognized him. 'So you have come,' she said.

She turned and he followed her. They crossed the courtyard, and Babu Ram saw the old man. He was lying on a low bed in the covered part of the courtyard. In front of him, on the ground, sat a little boy. The old man was saying, 'The hunter was so ugly that the birds all flew away at the sight of him. His eyes were bloodshot and he was flat of hand and foot and he carried a big, big club with spikes on it. . . .' The little boy sat quite still, his hands laid folded on his bare knees, and he was looking up into the old man's face with his eyes stretched wide and his teeth biting into his lower lip. Babu Ram stood still and looked at them, and his heart beat high. 'O Ram, O great Ram!' came triumphant voices from the temple; the cymbals danced and jingled – 'O Ram, O great Ram!' Suddenly Babu Ram knew that God would give him a son – perhaps had already given him one – who would sit like this little boy and listen to the old man telling stories. Waves of happiness passed over him, and he trembled.

The woman, seeing him look at the old man, also stopped, with her hand laid on her hip, and said, 'That is all he is good for – to lie all day on a bed and fill the heads of children with nonsense.'

'Like a tiger he came,' the old man was saying, 'very, very softly, and he held his terrible club in his hand and his teeth which were very sharp were bared like a tiger's.' He demonstrated these bared teeth and the little boy watched him.

'And to eat,' said the woman. 'How he can eat! O my God and fathers, how he can eat!' and she put up her hands to clutch her head. The chanting stopped, so after one last joyous tinkle did the cymbals. Now the house seemed very still, with only the drone of the old man's voice telling his story.

Another woman appeared out of the inner room, an older woman, very short and very broad and waddling from side to side as she walked. She also said to Babu Ram, 'So you have come,' and he again joined his palms in greeting and said, 'How are you, sister.'

'I hear your wife is having her sixth,' she said; adding, 'Well, let us hope this time . . .' The younger woman put her hand in front of her mouth and laughed from behind it. 'Though there is my sister's brother-in-law's wife – Shanti-devi we call her,' the older woman said. 'She had nine daughters before she had a son.'

'Oh no,' Babu Ram said with an instinctive gesture of defence. He knew this could not happen to him. He knew that his wife was about to give or had already given birth to a boy. God had spoken to him and promised him, through the chanting in the temple and the tinkling of tiny cymbals.

'One can never tell,' said the old woman. 'These things are in the hands of God. To some He gives and to some He does not give – it is so in life. O Lord,' she sighed.

To some He gives, thought Babu Ram and felt himself swelling with triumph. And now he wanted to hurry home, with the old man, to see how God had given to him.

'Like a great king he is lying there,' said the older woman, jerking her head towards the old man. 'The good-for-nothing.'

'Yesterday he ate up all the halwa again,' said the younger woman. 'What is it he has inside him – a pit or a stomach?'

'A curse on him,' said the old woman. They spoke loud enough for the old man to hear; but he went on droning his story without any change of expression – 'His terrible net was spread, and there he crouched, club in hand, and with a wicked, vicious look on his wicked, vicious face.' Babu Ram remembered how it had been the same in his own house; the women had cursed and the old man had calmly carried on, eating, sleeping, telling stories, as if he never as much as heard them. He had been a poor relation all his life and had learned how to live as one.

Babu Ram turned to him and said, 'You are coming?'

The old man gave no indication of having heard but continued to tell his story to the little boy, whose eyes never left his face. Babu Ram sat down and watched them, which gave him a deep pleasure. It was as if he were looking into the future and seeing his own son sitting thus listening to the old man. The two women continued to talk – about how necessary it was for a man to have a son, and about how much the old man ate and how lazy he was and good-for-

nothing – but Babu Ram hardly heard them. With his head
inclined to one side and a tender smile on his face, he sat
watching the old man and the boy.

At last the story was finished and the boy asked, 'That is
all?' and the old man answered, 'That is all.' Then he got
up from his bed, removed the rug on which he had been
lying, pulled out a bundle from under the bed and wrapped
it in the rug. He was ready.

Babu Ram jumped up. Suddenly he was in a great hurry
to get home, so that his farewell greetings to the women
were rather perfunctory. 'Well,' said the older woman, 'but
you have taken a great burden from our backs.' 'Like a
deliverer you have come,' said the younger woman. The
old man, his bundle under his arm, quietly followed Babu
Ram out of the house. He had some difficulty keeping up
with him, for Babu Ram was in such a hurry that he was
almost skipping on his plump little legs. They found a cycle
rickshaw and sat down in the seat at the back. 'Quickly!'
Babu Ram told the driver. 'Go quickly!' He couldn't wait
to get home and hold his son in his arms. The smile with
which he had watched the old man and the boy was still on
his face. 'Go faster,' he said from time to time. The rickshaw
driver clenched his teeth and put all his weight on to the
pedals of the cycle; perspiration trickled down his neck into
his torn and dirty vest. The old man sat holding his bundle
on his knees, enjoying the drive.

But when they reached the house, Babu Ram's haste left
him, and he walked up the stairs very slowly. All his elation,
all his certainty had gone; now he felt only rather afraid
and would even have liked to go away. There were no more
busy women rushing about, so he knew it was all finished.
Subdued voices came from the room where the birth had
taken place. Beckoning to the old man to follow him, he

went in, softly and timidly. A group of women were squatting on the floor, eating out of brass bowls; a few others were sitting on the bed on which his wife lay asleep with her head turned sideways and her hair straggling loose on her pillow. Next to the bed stood the cradle. Nobody said anything, so he knew it was another girl.

At last one of the women got up and took the baby out of the cradle and put it into his arms. Another woman said, 'We must welcome what God has given us,' so then everybody sighed and said, 'It is a gift from God,' and sighed again. Babu Ram looked down at his new baby. It was turning its head from side to side, with the mouth round and open like a little bird's; its neck too was scraggy like a little bird's. The old man bent forward and smiled a wide, toothless smile at the baby and clicked his fingers at it and made tender noises with his tongue. Then he looked at Babu Ram and smiled some more and nodded. So Babu Ram also smiled and began to rock the baby to and fro on his hands. 'Careful – what are you doing?' the women shouted, but the old man wagged his head and cackled with approval.

MY FIRST MARRIAGE

LAST week Rahul went on a hunger-strike. He didn't have
to suffer long – his family got very frightened (he is the only
son) and by the second day they were ready to do anything
he wanted, even to let him marry me. So he had a big meal,
and then he came to tell me of his achievement. He was so
proud and happy that I too pretended to be happy. Now his
father and Daddy are friends again, and they sit downstairs
in the study and talk together about their university days in
England. His mother too comes to the house, and yesterday
his married sister Kamla paid me a visit. The last time I had
met Kamla was when she told me all those things on their
veranda, but neither of us seemed to have any recollection
of that. Instead we had a very nice conversation about her
husband's promotion and the annual flower show for which
she had been asked to organize a raffle. Mama walks
around the house looking pleased with herself and humming
snatches of the national anthem (out of tune – she is completely unmusical). No one ever mentions M. any more.

It is two years now since he went away. I don't know
where he is or what he is doing. Perhaps he is meditating
somewhere in the Himalayas, or wandering by the banks of
the Ganges with an orange robe and a begging-bowl; or
perhaps he is just living in another town, trying to start a
newspaper or a school. Sometimes I ask myself: can there
really have been such a man? But it is not a question to
which I require any answer.

The first time I saw M., I was just going out to tennis

with Rahul. I hardly glanced at him – he was just one of the people who came to see Daddy. But he returned many times, and I heard Daddy say: 'That young man is a nuisance.' 'Of course,' said Mama in a sarcastic way, 'you can never say no to anyone.' Daddy looked shy: it was true, he found it difficult to refuse people. He is the Director of Education, and because it is an important position, people are always coming, both to the house and to his office, to ask him to do something for them. Mostly there is nothing he can do, but because he is so nice and polite to them, they keep coming again. Then often Mama steps in.

One day, just as I was going out to Rahul's house, I heard her shouting outside the door of the study. 'The Director is a busy man!' she was shouting. She had her back against the door and held her arms stretched out; M. stood in front of her, and his head was lowered. 'Day after day you come and eat his life up!' she said.

I feel very embarrassed when I hear Mama shouting at people, so I went away quickly. But when I was walking down the road, he suddenly came behind me. He said, 'Why are you walking so fast?'

I said nothing. I thought it was very rude of him to speak to me at all.

'You are running away,' he said.

Then in spite of myself I had to laugh: 'From what?'

'From the Real,' he said, and he spoke so seriously that I was impressed and stood still in the middle of the road and looked at him.

He was not really young – not young like I am, or like Rahul. His hair was already going grey and he had lines round his eyes. But what eyes they were, how full of wisdom and experience! And he was looking at me with them. I can't describe how I felt suddenly.

He said he wanted Daddy to open a new department in the university. A department for moral training. He explained the scheme to me and we both stood still in the road. His eyes glowed. I understood at once; of course, not everything – I am not a brilliant person such as he – but I understood it was important and even grand. Here were many new ideas, which made life seem quite different. I began to see that I had been living wrongly because I had been brought up to think wrongly. Everything I thought important, and Daddy and Mama and Rahul and everyone, was not important: these were the frivolities of life we were caught up in. For the first time someone was explaining to me the nature of reality. I promised to help him and to speak to Daddy. I was excited and couldn't stop thinking of everything he had said and the way he had said it.

He often telephoned. I waited for his calls and was impatient and restless till they came. But I was also a little ashamed to talk to him because I could not tell him that I had succeeded. I spoke to Daddy many times. I said, 'Education is no use without a firm moral basis.'

'How philosophical my little girl is getting,' Daddy said and smiled and was pleased that I was taking an interest in higher things.

Mama said, 'Don't talk so much; it's not nice in a young girl.'

When M. telephoned I could only say, 'I'm trying.'

'You are not trying!' he said; he spoke sternly to me. 'You are thinking of your own pleasures only, of your tennis and games.'

He was right – I often played tennis, and now that my examinations were finished, I spent a lot of time at the Club and went to the cinema and read novels. When he spoke to me, I realized all that was wrong; so that every time he telephoned I was thoughtful for many hours afterwards and when Rahul came to fetch me for tennis, I said I had a headache.

But I tried to explain to Rahul. He listened carefully; Rahul listens carefully to everything I say. He becomes very serious, and his eyes, which are already very large, become even larger. He looks so sweet then, just as he did when he was a little boy. I remember Rahul as a little boy, for we always played together. His father and Daddy were great friends, almost like brothers. So Rahul and I grew up together, and later it was decided we would be married. Everyone was happy: I also, and Rahul. We were to be married quite soon, for we had both finished our college and Rahul's father had already got him a good job in a business firm, with very fine prospects.

'You see, Rahul, we live in nice houses and have nice clothes and good education and everything, and all the time we don't know what reality is.'

Rahul frowned a bit, the way he used to do over his sums when they were difficult; but he nodded and looked at me with his big sweet eyes and was ready to listen to everything else I would tell him. Rahul has very smooth cheeks and they are a little bit pink because he is so healthy.

One day when M. telephoned he asked me to go and meet him. At first I tried to say no, but I knew I really wanted to go. He called me to a coffee-house I had never been to before, and I felt shy when going in – there were many men and no girls at all. Everyone looked at me; some of them may have been students from the university and perhaps they knew me. It was noisy in there and full of smoke and smell of fritters and chutney. The tablecloths were dirty and so were the bearers' uniforms. But he was there, waiting for me. I had often tried to recall his face but I never could:

now I saw it and – of course, of course, I cried to myself, that was how it was, how could I forget.

Then I began to meet him every day. Sometimes we met in that coffee-house, at other times in a little park where there was a broken swing and an old tomb and clerks came to eat their lunch out of tiffin-carriers. It was the end of winter and the sky was pale blue with little white lines on it and the sun was just beginning to get hot again and there were scarlet creepers all over the tomb and green parrots flew about. When I went home, I would lie on the bed in my room and think. Rahul came and I said I had a head-ache. I hardly knew anything anyone was saying. I ate very little. Mama often came into my room and asked, 'Where did you go today?' She was very sweet and gentle, the way she always is when she wants to find out something from you. I would tell her anything that came into my head – an old college friend had come from Poona, we had been to the cinema together – 'Which cinema?' Mama said, still sweet and gentle and tidying the handkerchiefs in my drawer. I would even tell her the story of the film I had not seen. 'Tomorrow I'm meeting her again.' 'No, tomorrow I want you to come with me to Meena auntie —'

It began to be difficult to get out of the house. Mama watched me every minute, and when she saw me ready to leave, she stood in the doorway: 'Today you are coming with me.'

'I told you, I have to meet —'

'You are coming with me!'

We were both angry and shouted. Daddy came out of the study. He told Mama, 'She is not a child. . . .'

Then Mama started to shout at him and I ran out of the house and did not look back, though I could hear her calling me.

When I told M., he said, 'You had better come with me.'
I also saw there was no other way. On Friday afternoons
Mama goes to a committee meeting of the All-India Ladies'
Council, so that was the best time. I bundled up all my
clothes and jewels in a sheet and I walked out of the house.
Faqir Chand, our butler, saw me, but he said nothing –
probably he thought I was sending my clothes to the
washerman. M. was waiting for me in a tonga by the post
office and he helped me climb up and sit beside him; the
tonga was a very old and shaky one, and the driver was also
old and so was the horse. We went very slowly, first by the
river, past the Fort and through all the bazaars, he and I
sitting side by side at the back of the tonga with my bundle
between us.

We had such a strange wedding. I laugh even now when
I think of it. He had a friend who was a sign-painter and
had a workshop on the other side of the river. The workshop
was really only a shed, but they made it very nice – they
turned all the signboards to the wall and they hung my
saris over them and over the saris they hung flower garlands.
It looked really artistic. They also bought sweetmeats and
nuts and put them on a long table which they had borrowed
from a carpenter. Several friends of his came and quite a
lot of people who lived in sheds and huts near by. There
was a priest and a fire was lit and we sat in front of it and
the priest chanted the holy verses. I was feeling very hot
because of the fire and of course my face was completely
covered by the sari. It wasn't a proper wedding sari, but
my own old red sari which I had last worn when Mama
gave a tea-party for the professors' wives in our drawing-
room, with cakes from Wenger's.

M. got very impatient, he kept telling the priest, 'Now hurry hurry, we have heard all that before.'

The priest was offended and said, 'These are all holy words.'

I couldn't help laughing under my sari, even though I was crying at the same time because I was thinking of Daddy and Rahul and Mama.

There was a quarrel – his friends also told him to keep quiet and let the priest say his verses in the proper manner, and he got angry and shouted, 'Is it my marriage or yours?'

At last it was finished and we were married and everyone ate sweetmeats and nuts, even people who just wandered in from the road and whom no one knew.

We stayed a few days with his friend. There was a little room built out of planks just off the workshop and in that we all slept at night, rolled up in blankets. In the day, when the friend painted signs, we stayed in the room by ourselves, M. and I, and no one came in to disturb us. When he slept, I would look at him and look; I studied all the lines on his face. After I had looked my fill, I would shut my eyes and try and see his face in my mind, and when I opened them again, there he was really, his real face, and I cried out loud with joy.

After some days we went on a bus to Niripat. The journey was four hours long and the bus was crowded with farmers and labourers and many old women carrying little bundles. There was a strong smell of poor people who can't afford to change their clothes very often and of the food which the old women ate out of their bundles and the petrol from the bus. I began to feel a little sick. I often get car-sick: when we used to drive up to Naini Tal for the summer holidays, Daddy always had to stop the car several times so that I could go out and take fresh air; and Mama would give me lemon-drops to suck and rub my temples with eau-de-cologne.

In Niripat we stayed with M.'s cousin, who had a little brick house just outside the town. They were a big family, and the women lived in one side of the house, in a little set of dark rooms with only metal trunks and beds in them, and the men on the other side. But I ran all over the house; I was singing and laughing all the time. In the evenings I sat with the men and listened to them talking about religion and philosophy and their business (they had a grinding-mill); and during the day I helped the women with their household work. M. and I went out for walks and sometimes we went swimming in a pond. The women of the house teased me a lot because I liked M. so much. 'But look at him,' they said, 'he is so dark; and see! his hair is going grey like an old man's.' Or, 'He is just a loafer – it is only talking with him and never any work.' I pretended to be annoyed with them (of course, I knew they were only joking) and that made them laugh more than ever. One of them said, 'Now it is very fine, but just wait, in the end her state will be the same as Savitri's.'

'Savitri?' I said.

So that was how I first heard about Savitri and the children. At first I was unhappy, but M. explained everything. He had been married very young and to a simple girl from a village. After some years he left her. She understood it was necessary for him to leave her because he had a task to fulfil in the world in which she could not help him. She went back to her parents, with the children. She was happy now, because she saw it was her duty to stay at home and look after the children and lead the good, simple, self-sacrificing life of a mother. He talked of her with affection:

she was patient and good. I too learned to love her. I thought of her in the village, with the children, quietly doing her household tasks; early in the mornings and in the evenings she said her prayers. So her life passed. He had gone to see her a few times and she had welcomed him and been glad; but when he went away again, she never tried to keep him. I thought how it would be if he went away from me, but I could not even bear the idea. My heart hurt terribly and I stifled a cry. From that I saw how much nobler and more advanced Savitri was than I; and I hoped that, if the time ever came, I too could be strong like her. But not yet. Not yet. We sold my pearl brooch and sent money to her; he always sent money to her when he had it. Once he said of her: 'She is a candle burning in a window of the world,' and that was how I always thought of her – as a candle burning for him with a humble flame.

I had not yet written to Daddy and Mama, but I wrote to Rahul. I wrote, 'Everything is for the best, Rahul. I often think about you. Please tell everyone that I am all right and happy.' M. and I went to the post office together to buy a stamp and post the letter. On the way back he said, 'You must write to your father also. He must listen to our ideas.' How proud I was when he said *our* ideas.

Daddy and Mama came to Niripat. Daddy sent me a letter in which it said they were waiting for me at the Victoria Hotel. M. took me there, and then went away; he said I must talk to them and explain everything. The Victoria Hotel is the only hotel in Niripat and it is not very grand – it is certainly not the sort of hotel in which Mama is used to staying. In front there is the Victoria Restaurant where meals can be had at a reduced rate on a monthly basis; there is an open passage at the side which leads to the hotel rooms. Some of the guests had pulled their beds out into the passage and were sitting on them: I noticed a very fat man in a dhoti and an undervest saying his prayers. But Daddy and Mama were inside their room.

It was a very small room with two big beds in it and a table with a blue cotton tablecloth in the middle. Mama was lying on one of the beds; she was crying, and when I came in, she cried more. Daddy and I embraced each other, but Mama turned her face away and pressed her eyes with her handkerchief and the tears rolled right down into her blouse. It made me impatient to see her like that: every mother must part with her daughter some time, so what was there to cry about? I squeezed Daddy's hands, to show him how happy I was, but then he too turned his face away from me and he coughed. Here we were meeting after so many days, and they were both behaving in a ridiculous manner. I spoke to them quite sharply: 'Every individual being must choose his own life and I have chosen mine.'

'Don't, darling,' Daddy said as if something were hurting him.

Mama suddenly shouted, 'You are my shame and disgrace!'

'Quietly, quietly,' Daddy said.

I felt like shouting back at her, but I controlled myself; I had not come there to quarrel with her, even if she had come to quarrel with me. I was a wiser person now than I had been. So I only said: 'There are aspects of life which you will never grasp.'

A little servant-boy came in with tea on a tray. Mama sat up on the bed – she is always very keen on her tea – but after a while she sank back again and said in a fainting sort of voice, 'There is something dirty in the milk.' I had a look and there were only bits of straw, from the cowshed, which I fished out easily with a tea-spoon.

Daddy gave a big sigh and said, 'You had better let me speak with the young man.'

So then I was happy again: I knew that when Daddy really spoke to him and got to know him, he would soon realize what sort of a person M. was and everything would be all right.

And everything was all right. It was true, Daddy couldn't start the department of moral training for him, as we had hoped, because the university didn't have enough funds for a new department; and also, Daddy said, he couldn't get him an academic post because M. didn't have the necessary qualifications. (How stupid are these rules and regulations! Here was a wonderful gifted person like M., with great ideas and wide experience of life, who had so much to pass on; yet he had to take a backward place to some poor little M.A. or Ph.D. who knows nothing of life at all except what he has read in other people's books.) So all Daddy could do was get him a post as secretary to one of the college principals; and I think it was very nice of M. to accept it, because it was not the sort of post a person such as he had a right to expect. But he was always like that: he knew nothing of petty pride and never stood on his dignity, unlike many other people who have really no dignity at all to stand on.

I was sorry to leave Niripat where I had been so happy with everyone and to go home again. But of course it was different now, because M. was with me. We had the big guest-room at the back of the house and at night we made our beds out on the lawn. Sometimes I thought how funny it was – only a few weeks ago Mama had tried to turn him out of the house and here he was back in the best guest-room.

It is true that the wheel of fate has many unexpected revolutions. I think he quite liked living in the house, though I was afraid at first he would feel stifled with so many servants and all that furniture and carpets and clocks and Mama's china dinner-services. But he was too great in soul to be bothered by these trivial things; he transcended them and led his life and thought his thoughts in the same way as he would have done if he had been living in some little hut in the jungle.

If only Mama had had a different character. But she is too sunk in her own social station and habits to be able to look out and appreciate anything higher. She thinks if a person has not been abroad and doesn't wear suits and open doors for ladies, he is an inferior type of person. If M. had tried, I know he could have used a knife and fork quite as well as Mama or anyone, but why should he have tried? And there were other things like not making a noise when you drink your tea, which are just trivial little conventions we should all rise above. I often tried to explain this to Mama but I could never make her understand. So it became often quite embarrassing at meal-times, with Mama looking at M. and pretending she couldn't eat her own food on account of the way he was eating his. M. of course never noticed, and I felt so ashamed of Mama that in the end I also refused to use any cutlery and ate with my hands. Daddy never said anything – in fact, Daddy said very little at all nowadays, and spent long hours in his office and went to a lot of meetings and, when he came home, he only sat in his study and did not come out to talk to us.

I often thought about Rahul. He had never answered my letter and when I tried to telephone, they said he was not at home. But I wanted very much to see him; there were so many things I had to tell him about. So one day I went to his house. The servants made me wait on the veranda and then Rahul's married sister Kamla came out. Kamla is a very ambitious person and she is always scheming for her husband's promotion (he is in the Ministry of Defence) so that she can take precedence over the other wives in his department. I was not surprised at the way she talked to me. I know a person like Kamla will always think only petty thoughts and doesn't understand that there is anything transcending the everyday life in which she is sunk up to her ears. So I let her say what she wanted and when she told me to go away, I went. When Mama found out that I had been to Rahul's house, she was furious. 'All right, so you have lost all pride for yourself, but for your family – at least think of us!' At the word pride I laughed out loud: Mama's ideas of pride were so different from mine and M.'s. But I was sorry that they wouldn't let me see Rahul.

M. went out every day, and I thought he went to his job in the university. But one day Daddy called me into his study and he said that M. had lost his job because he hadn't been going there for weeks. I had a little shock at first, but then I thought it is all right, whatever he wants to do is all right; and anyway, it hadn't been a suitable post for him in the first place. I told Daddy so.

Daddy played with his silver paper-knife and he didn't look at me at all; then he said, 'You know he has been married before?' and still he didn't look at me.

I don't know how Daddy found out – I suppose he must have been making inquiries, it is the sort of thing people in our station of life always do about other people, we are so mistrustful – but I answered him quite calmly. I tried to explain to him about Savitri.

After a while Daddy said, 'I only wanted you to know

that your marriage is not legal and can be dissolved any time you want.'

Then I told him that marriages are not made in the sight of the law but in the sight of God, and that in the sight of God both Savitri and I were married to M., she there and I here. Daddy turned his head away and looked out of the window.

M. told me that he wanted to start a school and that he could do so if Daddy got him a grant from the Ministry. I thought it was a very exciting idea and we talked a lot about it that night, as we lay together on our beds. He had many wonderful ideas about how a school should be run and said that the children should be taught to follow only their instincts which would lead them to the highest Good. He talked so beautifully, like a prophet, a saint. I could hardly sleep all night, and first thing in the morning I talked to Daddy. Unfortunately Mama was listening at the door – she has a bad habit of doing that – and suddenly she came bursting in. 'Why don't you leave your father alone?' she cried. 'Isn't it enough that we give you both food and shelter?'

I said, 'Mama please, I'm talking important business with Daddy.'

She began to say all sorts of things about M. and why he had married me. Daddy tried to keep her quiet but she was beyond herself by that time, so I just covered my ears with my hands and ran out. She came after me, still shouting these horrible things.

There in the hall was M., and when I tried to run past him, he stopped me and took my hands from my ears and made me listen to everything Mama was saying. She got more and more furious, and then she went into one of her hysterical fits, in which she throws herself down and beats her head on the floor and tears at her clothes. Daddy tried to lift her up, but of course she is too heavy for him. She went on screaming and shouting at M.

M. said, 'Go and get your things,' so I went and wrapped everything up in the sheet again, his things and mine, and he slung the bundle over his shoulder and went out of the house, with me walking behind him.

I hoped we would go back to Niripat, but he wanted to stay in the city because he had several schemes in mind – there was the school, and he also had hopes of starting a newspaper in which he could print all his ideas. So he had to go round and see a lot of people, in Ministries and so on. Sometimes he got quite discouraged because it was so difficult to make people understand. Then he looked tired and the lines on his face became very deep and I felt such love and pity for him. But he had great inner strength, and next day he always started on his rounds again, as fresh and hopeful as before.

We had no proper home at that time, but lived in several places. There was the sign-painter, and another friend had a bookshop in one of the government markets with a little room at the back where we could stay with him; and once we found a model house which was left over from a low-cost housing exhibition and we lived in that till workmen came to tear it down. There were plenty of places where we could stay for a few days or even weeks. In the evenings there were always many friends and all sat and discussed their ideas, and some of them recited poetry or played the flute, so that sometimes we didn't go to sleep at all. We never had any worries about money – M. said if one doesn't think about money, one doesn't need it, and how true that is.

Daddy sent me a cheque every month, care of the friend who kept the bookshop, and we still had some of my jewellery which we could sell whenever we wanted; so there was even money to send to Savitri and the children.

Once I met Rahul, quite by chance. That was at the time when we had just moved out of the exhibition house. M. had to go to one of the Ministries to see an Under-Secretary, and I was taking our bundle to an orphanage, run by a friend of M.'s, where we were going to stay. I was waiting for a bus, holding the bundle; it wasn't heavy at all any more, so there was no need to take a tonga. Rahul came out of a music-shop with some records which he had just bought (he is very fond of dance-records – how often we have danced together to his gramophone!) I called to him and when he didn't hear me, I went up to him. He lowered his eyes and wouldn't look at me and hardly greeted me.

'Rahul,' I said in the stern voice I always use with him when I think he is misbehaving.

'Why did you do it?' he said. 'My family are very angry with you and I'm also angry.' He sulked, but he looked so sweet; he still had his pink cheeks.

'If you have your car, you can give me a lift,' I said. Rahul is always a gentleman, and he even carried my bundle for me to his car.

It took us a long time to find the orphanage – it was right at the back of the Fatehpuri mosque somewhere – so there was plenty of time for me to talk to him. He listened quite quietly, driving the car through all that traffic. When at last we found the orphanage and I was ready to get out, he said, 'Don't go yet.' I stayed with him for a while, even though the car was parked very awkwardly in that crowded alley-way, and men with barrows swore at us because they could not get past.

Soon afterwards a friend of M.'s who was in the railways got transferred, and as he lived in a house with a very low rent, it was a good opportunity for us and we took it over from him. There were two rooms and a little yard at the back, and upstairs two families were living. Daddy used to send a cheque for the rent. I cooked for us and cleaned the house and talked with the families upstairs, while M. went out to see people about his ideas. But after a time he began to go out less and less, and he became depressed; he said the world had rejected him because he was not strong enough yet. Now it was his task to purify himself and make himself stronger. He stayed at home and meditated. A strange change came over him. Most of the time he sat in one of our rooms, in a corner of the floor, by himself and he wouldn't let me come in. Sometimes I heard him singing to himself and shouting – he made such strange noises, almost like an animal. For days he ate nothing at all and, when I tried to coax him, he upset the food I had brought and threw it on the floor. I tried to be patient and bear and understand everything.

His friends stopped coming and he hardly ever left that little room for two months. Then he started going out by himself – I never knew where and could not ask him. He had an expression on his face as if he were listening for something, so that one felt one couldn't disturb him. When he talked to me, he talked as if he was someone else and I was someone else. At night I slept in the yard at the back with the families from upstairs, who were always kind to me.

Then visitors began to come for him – not his old friends, but quite new people whom I had never seen before. They sat with him in the little room and I could hear him talking to them. At first only a few men used to come, but then more and more came, and women too. I also sat in the room sometimes and listened to him talk; he told strange stories about parrots and princes and tigers in the jungle, all of which had some deep meaning. When the people understood the deep meaning, they all exclaimed with pleasure and said God was speaking through his mouth.

Now they began to bring us gifts of food and money and clothes and even jewellery. M. never took any notice, and I just piled the things in the other room which was soon very crowded. We ate the food and I also gave it to the families upstairs, but there was still plenty left over, and at night someone used to come from the beggars' home to take it away. I sent a lot of money to Savitri. The house was always full of people now, and they spilled over into the yard and out into the street. More and more women came – most of them were old but there were some young ones too, and the young ones were even more fervent and religious than the old ones. There was one plump and pretty young widow, who was always dressed very nicely and came every day. She said she was going mad with love of God and needed words of solace and comfort from M. She touched his feet and implored him to relieve her, and when he took no notice of her, she shook him and tugged at his clothes, so that he became quite angry.

Mama often came to see me. In the beginning she was very disgusted with the house and the way we lived and everything, but afterwards, when she saw how many people came and all the things they brought and how they respected M., she kept quiet on that subject. Now she only said, 'Who knows what is to become of it all?' Mama is not really a religious person, but she has a lot of superstitions. When holy men come begging to her house, she always gives them something – not because of their holiness, but because she is afraid they will curse her and bring the evil eye on us all. She no longer said anything bad about M., and when she talked about him, she didn't say 'that one' as she used to, but always 'He'. Once or twice she went and sat with the other people in the little room in which he was, and when she came out, she looked so grave and thoughtful that I had to laugh.

Rahul also visited me. At first he was stiff and sulky, as if he were doing me a favour by coming; but then he began to talk, all about how lonely he was and how his family were trying to persuade him to marry girls he didn't like. I felt sorry for him – I knew it is always difficult for him to make friends and he has never really had anyone except me. I let him talk, and he kept coming again and again. There was a little space with a roof of asbestos sheet over it in the yard, where I did my cooking, and it was here that Rahul and I sat. It was not a very private place because of all the people in the yard, waiting to see M., but Rahul soon got used to it and talked just as he would have done if we had been sitting in Mama's drawing-room. He was very melancholy, and when he had finished telling me about how lonely he was, he only sat and looked at me with big sad eyes. So I let him help me with the cooking – at first he only sifted the rice and lentils, but after a time I let him do some real cooking and he enjoyed it terribly. He would make all sorts of things – fritters and potato cakes and horse-radish pancakes – and they were really delicious. We ate some ourselves and the rest we sent to the beggars' home.

There were always a few young men who stayed at night and slept outside the door of the room where M. was. I often heard him get up in the night and walk up and down; and sometimes he shouted at the young men sleeping outside his door, 'Go home!' and he kicked them with his foot, he was so impatient and angry with them. He was often angry nowadays. I heard him shouting at people and scolding them for coming to pester him. When he scolded them, they said he was right to do so, because they were bad, sinful people; but they did not go away and, on the contrary, even more came.

One night I felt someone shaking me to wake up. I opened my eyes and it was M. I jumped up at once and we went out into the street together and sat on a doorstep. Here and there people were sleeping on the sidewalk or on the platforms of shuttered shops. It was very dark and quiet. Only sometimes someone coughed in his sleep or there was a watchman's cry and the tap of his stick. M. said, 'Soon I shall have to go away.'

Then I knew that the time I had always feared was near.

He said, 'It will be best for you to go home again.' He spoke very practically, and with gentleness and great concern for me.

But I didn't want to think about what I was going to do. For the moment I wanted it to be only now – always night and people always sleeping and he and I sitting together like this on the doorstep for ever and ever.

The plump young widow still came every day and every day in a different sari, and she made such scenes that in the end M. forbade her to come any more. So she hung about outside in the yard for a few days, and then she started peeping into his room and after that she crept in behind the others and sat quietly at the back; till finally she showed herself to him quite openly and even began to makes scenes again. 'Have pity!' she cried. 'God is eating me up!' At last he quite lost his temper with her. He took off his slipper and began to beat her with it and when she ran away, screaming and clutching her sari about her, he ran after her, brandishing his slipper. They were a funny sight. He pursued her right out into the street, and then he turned back and began to chase all the other people out of the house. He scattered them right and left, beating at them with his slipper, and cursing and scolding. Everyone ran away very fast – even Rahul, who had been cooking potato cakes, made off in a great fright. When they had all gone, M. returned to his room and locked the door behind him. He looked hot and angry.

And next day he was gone. People came as usual that day but when they realized he was no longer there, they went away again and also took their gifts back with them. That night the men from the beggars' home were disappointed. I stayed on by myself, it didn't matter to me where I was. Sometimes I sat in one of the rooms, sometimes I walked up and down. The families from upstairs tried to make me eat and sleep, but I heard nothing of what they said. I don't remember much about that time. Later Daddy came to take me away. For the last time I tied my things up in a sheet and I went with him.

I think sometimes of Savitri, and I wonder whether I too am like her now – a candle burning for him in a window of the world. I am patient and inwardly calm and lead the life that has been appointed for me. I play tennis again and I go out to tea and garden-parties with Mama, and Rahul and I often dance to the gramophone. Probably I shall marry Rahul quite soon. I laugh and talk just as much as I used to and Mama says I am too frivolous, but Daddy smiles and encourages me. Mama has had a lot of new pieces of jewellery made for me to replace the ones I sold; she and I keep on quarrelling as before.

I still try and see his face in my mind, and I never succeed. But I know – and that is how I can go on living the way I do, and even enjoy my life and be glad – that one day I shall succeed and I shall see that face as it really is. But whose face it is I shall see in that hour of happiness – and indeed, whose face it is I look for with such longing – is not quite clear to me.